I0668094

Vlad-Handing

SILVER HILLS COZY MYSTERIES, Volume 7

Sam Cheever

Published by Electric Prose Publications, 2018.

This is a work of fiction. Similarities to real people, places, or events are entirely coincidental.

VLAD-HANDING

First edition. February 28, 2018.

Written by Sam Cheever.

COME TO SILVER HILLS. *Where an old nemesis can lead to new trouble and murder is a line item in a business plan.*

Vlad Newsome isn't exactly known as a people person. He's really more contentious than convivial.

But something's changed with him, and Flo and Agnes are suspicious.

Vlad's suddenly "peopling". He's shaking hands and even curving his thin lips upward at times in a terrifying imitation of a smile.

Could it be he's turning over a new leaf? Is he facing a life-changing event that's made him grow as a person?

Nah...

He's up to something. And Flo and Agnes are determined to find out what.

When a woman who had a beef with the reprehensible creature of the night known as Vlad Newsome turns up dead in her home...Vlad appears to be the culprit behind her murder.

Silver City PD certainly believe he's guilty. But Vlad insists he's innocent. It's going to be up to Flo and Co. to solve the murder and find the "real" killer. Unfortunately for everyone involved, the ladies aren't totally certain Vlad isn't the murderer.

Will Flo and Co. walk away...leave Vlad to defend himself? If you believe that you haven't been paying attention.

After all, this *is* Flo and Agnes!

Sam doesn't give away a lot of books. But she values her readers and, to show it, she's gifting you a copy of a fun book just for signing up for her newsletter!

<u>SIGN UP HERE!</u>[1]

<u>https://samcheever.com/newsletter/</u>

---

1. https://samcheever.com/newsletter/

CHAPTER ONE

"MAYBE SOMEBODY DIED," Agnes offered.

Flo rolled her eyes and pulled a spiky branch up to cover her face. "I hope not, since they're all laughing."

Agnes's round face folded into a frown. "In some cultures, death is celebrated."

"While I realize being a vampire could be considered another culture...I doubt any of Vlad's victims or their families would celebrate death by fang." Flo ducked, pulling the branch with her, as the goth version of a night manager skimmed a look her way. Regrettably, her movement totally exposed her fellow stalker.

Agnes gulped loudly as Vladwick Newsome fixed his black, deadly gaze on her, clearly miffed. "He saw me, Flo."

Another man approached Vlad and, unbelievably, the usually unfriendly night manager offered the tall, tough-looking man his hand. They shook vigorously and Vlad actually leaned close, whispering something to the other man that made him smile.

"What the?" Agnes stood up, glaring across the street until Vlad turned her way. Then he said something to his new friend and started toward them, his dark eyes flashing with anger.

Flo grabbed her friend's hand. "Come on. It's still daylight. His powers are weaker when the sun's up."

Snorting, Agnes let herself be dragged toward the street. "I almost wish he really was a vampire so that would be true."

Flo sighed. "Me too." They hurried across the street and headed toward home. "I think we just witnessed Vlad's attempt to foil our plans."

Agnes shrugged. "To tell you the truth, I'm okay with that. I really don't want to be a weekend manager."

"Why not?" Flo asked. "I'll admit the pay's not great but it would be nice to have a little extra income, wouldn't it?" Agnes didn't actually have *any* income at the moment. She was able to live at Silver Hills because of an inheritance from her parents, which was just enough to pay for her apartment there and not much else.

Her friend shrugged. "It's just..."

"Hey!" The snotty, strident voice assaulted them from across the street.

Flo grabbed Agnes' hand, pulling her into a faster walk. "Don't look back."

"We can't just ignore him," Agnes said as she began to turn.

Flo jerked her around. "Don't! He's just going to threaten you and Tolstoy with eviction again."

"Flo, you know he's going to do that anyway. He's going to be mad if I put my name in the hat for the manager's position."

"But if you get the job he won't be able to threaten you with that ever again," Flo reminded her.

She saw the moment the realization hit. Agnes' round, expressive face brightened in a smile. "You're right." To Flo's horror, Agnes stopped and turned as Vlad hurried closer. "What up, vamp?"

The cranky night manager curled his lip and oozed to a stop deep inside their comfort zone.

Flo took a step backward, glaring at him. "Vlad."

He gave her a smug grimace. "Annoying woman from the second floor."

Flo fought irritation. The man knew perfectly well who she was. He just liked to pretend she was so unimportant he couldn't remember her name. She clamped her lips down on the desire to give it to him again. It wouldn't make any difference and would allow him a win.

She was all about not giving Vlad Newsome a win.

He turned a piercing, nearly black gaze toward Agnes. Flo saw her friend twitch, her eyes widening as if she couldn't look away.

"He can't compel you with his gaze, Agnes."

Agnes chewed on her bottom lip. "Are you sure? I'm feeling kind of woozy."

"That's because you stopped breathing." Flo touched her friend's thick wrist. "Drop your eyes and breathe, fool."

Agnes didn't blink. Her eyes were so big Flo was afraid they might be stuck. "Agnes, a bug's going to fly into your eyes if you don't blink."

Agnes' mouth opened into a horrified "O". She hated when that happened. "I can't Flo, he's got me."

Vlad chuckled darkly, clearly enjoying Agnes' hysteria.

Flo reached out and punched him in the arm.

"Ow!" His smile died as he rubbed his skinny arm. "That hurt."

Fortunately, when he looked away, Agnes broke the spell she'd put on herself. She glared at him. "You won't stop me with your vampire ways," she told him angrily.

He shook his head. "You people are idiots. There is no such thing as vampires."

"That's exactly what a vampire would say when it was about to be outed," Agnes told him smugly.

Vlad shook his dark head but didn't give her a smarmy comeback.

Flo jerked her head toward the spot where they'd seen him actually conversing with Silver Hills residents. "You were talking to the Baccarat brothers. What are you up to, Vlad?" He'd never before bothered to speak to anyone unless he had to. The fact that he'd been laughing and glad-handing with three men from the third floor made her very suspicious.

"I don't believe my personal conversations are under your purview, woman from the second floor."

Flo growled a little before she caught herself. "You never speak to any of us. You're up to something and I promise you I'm going to find out what it is."

He stared at her, his dark gaze cold and dead like a shark's. Flo barely restrained from shuddering under that icy perusal. "I saw you two spying on me from behind the potted plant. You need to stop following me around or I'm going to speak to Detective Peters about a restraining order."

Flo's stomach did a little flip. He'd actually surprised her with that one. "We weren't following you around."

He lifted a slender black brow. "Oh? So, your story is you just happened to be skulking around behind that plant and I walked across your field of vision?"

Flo thought for a moment, wondering if she could sell that if she needed to. But of course, she'd never get that chance because she had Chatty Agnes for a best friend.

"For your information, we've never spied on you before. This was the first time."

"Not helping, Agnes," Flo murmured.

"But Flo's right. You *are* up to something and we're going to find out what it is."

Vlad crossed his arms over his scrawny chest. "Then I can expect more stalking?"

"Yes."

"No!"

Flo glared at her friend. Agnes lowered her brow and glared back. "He's not going to get away with this, Flo."

Vlad chuckled. "Get away with what, mutant? Having a conversation with friends on the street?"

Flo's first instinct was to laugh. The idea of Vladwick Newsome having friends was ludicrous. It wasn't even clear if his wife, Morty liked him.

Flo blinked. *Morty...* She grabbed Agnes' beefy arm. "We're going home. And you can rest assured we won't be peering at you through any more plants," she told him with a grim smile. "We won't need to."

She could feel his hostile glare on her back as they hoofed it toward Silver Hills. Flo knew what he was thinking and he was right. She smiled.

"Was that a threat?" he called after them.

Flo's smile widened. She merely threw a hand up and waved at him above her head.

"You look like Tolstoy after he caught that mouse last week," Agnes said.

Grimacing at the memory of mouse corpse on her welcome mat, Flo stepped up the pace in case Vlad decided to turn into mist and try to overtake them. "If the mouse represents that horrible man then, guilty as charged."

"What are you up to, Flo?"

She tugged the front door open and held it for her friend. "Nothing."

Agnes stepped through ahead of her. "I know that look on your face, Flo. That's not nothing."

Flo chuckled. "You're right. It's something." A reedy voice hailed them from the bar and they looked up to find Scarlett holding court with several of the singles and Roger Attles, Flo's sort of boyfriend. She waved as he stood up and motioned for her to join them. Always the gentleman.

"Come on, looks like happy hour started without us."

"You go ahead, hun. I'm going to the office. I'll be there in a minute."

"And there it is." Agnes heaved out a big sigh. "You'll tell me later?"

"Of course."

"Mm hm." Agnes shook her big head. "Between you and the blood sucker I just can't keep up."

Flo watched her friend walk across the room to a resounding cheer as the singles caught sight of her. Agnes did a little dance and they all broke out into a chorus of laughter.

Flo held her finger up to Roger and determinedly turned toward the door marked with an "Office" sign. If she was lucky

Morticia Newsome would be at her desk. And not out terrifying villagers or running from a pitchfork wielding mob.

Surprisingly, Morticia's drawn, narrow face wasn't the one that greeted Flo when she opened the door.

Richard Attles, the day manager at Silver Hills and son to Flo's kind of boyfriend, Roger, smiled up from the desk Morty usually haunted. "Afternoon, Mrs. Bee. What can I do you for?" He stood up and closed the folder he'd been perusing when she opened the door

"I was hoping to speak with Morty."

Richard walked around the oversized wood desk and sat down on the front edge, crossing his arms over his chest. "She's not here yet. I expect her any minute." He cocked his head when Flo frowned. "Is everything all right?"

She knew he had to be surprised that Flo was looking for Morty. Despite the fact that Flo had helped Morty on a kidnapping-cultist case recently, the two of them could hardly be considered besties. "I was hoping to find out how the search was going for the weekend manager." To Flo's surprise, the goth twins, Vlad and Morty, had volunteered to vet out and hire the new manager themselves. Or at least give recommendations for who should be hired.

"They've been very closed lipped about it all." He glanced toward the folder on the desk. "I think it's going well. We've had lots of people come in for interviews."

She thought carefully for a moment before responding. Finally, she asked, "anybody promising?"

"Why do I get the impression you have a specific question you aren't asking me?"

"Probably because I do. Agnes and I just spotted Vlad downtown, schmoozing the Baccarat brothers from three."

Richard's light brown eyebrows shot skyward. "Schmoozing?"

"Yeah. That was my reaction too. He even shook their hands and I didn't see him pull out the sanitizer after he did."

"Vlad doesn't schmooze." He glanced at Flo and shook his head. "I don't need to tell you that, do I? If anybody understands how allergic the Newsomes are to peopling it's you."

"Amen and amen." She glanced toward the door and stepped closer, lowering her voice. "Are the Newsome's vying for the weekend job themselves?"

Richard frowned. "I hadn't even considered that. I'm not sure why they would, since the position is being filled to give the three of us some time off."

"But there's money attached to the job now."

"True. The extra money might be an inducement." He gave it another moment's thought and then shook his head. "I really doubt the board would give them the job. Vlad has to know that."

"Maybe they know someone they want to stuff into it, then?" One of the interesting aspects of the new hire was the board's insistence that the residents would have a vote in who they picked. What Richard was too kind to say was that, in a popularity contest, the Newsome's would be dead in the water. Unless they turned over a new leaf really fast. Or did some creative bribing. But if they'd made a deal with somebody to push the vote their way...well...Flo made it a point never to underestimate the gruesome twosome's criminal genius. "Do they seem partial to anyone in particular?"

"There was this one young woman..." His eyes went wide. "Now that I think on it, they did seem to know a lot about her."

"A relative, maybe?"

"Not unless she's a very distant relative. I don't think they've ever met her face to face. I've seen her and she's not the Newsomes' kind of people."

Grinning, Flo took his meaning. "You mean she probably wouldn't get offered a job in the next *Addam's Family* remake?"

"As Cousin Marilyn, maybe..."

"The ugly one..." Flo laughed. "Got it. Thanks, Richard."

"No problem. Hey, wasn't Agnes going to put in for the job?"

Flo opened the door and stood with it cracked only a couple of inches. "I've been working on her but she's resistant."

"Why? As popular as she is, she'd be a shoe in."

"That's what I keep telling her. Don't worry, I'll make sure she applies."

"Well hurry up. Applications are going to be cut off at the end of the week." He smiled. "I'd love to see Agnes get the job. She knows everybody and is well liked. And she comes fully equipped with a regulating mechanism."

"You mean me?"

Richard's grin widened. "See you later."

Shaking her head, Flo left the office chuckling. Richard was right. If Agnes got the job, Flo would be there to help and...guide...her through any difficulties she encountered. The residence would really be getting two managers for the price of one. Flo knew she should resent his expectation, but she liked Richard. He was good people. And he was a smart man. Flo would support her friend through whatever crisis Agnes might encounter as a weekend manager. She wouldn't have it any other way.

"Hey there, doll."

She looked up to find Roger heading her way, his long, lean form moving lithely across the entryway and his handsome face filled with pleasure. She got a warm jolt of happiness in the center of her chest upon seeing him. There was just something so wonderful about being with someone who was that pleased to cast eyes on you.

Especially someone as handsome and distinguished as Roger Attles.

"Hey yourself."

He captured her hand and lifted it to his lips, giving it a warm kiss that made her toes curl with pleasure. He nodded toward the office. "Is there a problem?"

"No. I was just trying to get the inside scoop on the weekend manager job."

He lifted bushy gray brows in surprise. "Are you considering taking it?"

"Not me. I'm trying to get Agnes to take it."

A cheer went up in the bar and they turned to find Agnes chugging the biggest beer Flo had ever seen. She sighed. "I must be crazy."

"You're not crazy at all, doll. Agnes would be a wonderful manager's assistant. People love her."

Flo turned a surprised glance his way. "Assistant? No, I'm trying to get her to take the manager's job."

Roger nodded. "Yes. And when something happens, who will she call for advice?"

Flo opened her mouth and then frowned, slamming her lips closed. "I'm not sure I like where everybody's thoughts are heading with this."

Roger chuckled. "It's a burden to always be the responsible one."

Another cheer drew their attention to the bar, where they found Agnes stuffing two hot dogs at once into her bulging cheeks.

Flo sighed. "I'm toast."

"More like Angel food cake, doll."

She flushed with pleasure.

The overhead lights flickered and everybody stilled, all eyes sliding to the front door.

It opened a beat later and Morty glided inside, her long, narrow feet seeming to ride above the floor on a current of air. The night manager turned a pinched, snotty look toward Flo and her blood-red lips pursed as if she'd sucked a lemon. She glided toward the office without so much as a word or a wave in Flo's direction. Directly behind her, the second half of the Newsome twosome floated through the door. Vlad's soulless gaze skimmed in her direction and he stopped, his thin lips forming into a smug smile.

A moment later Vlad inclined his chin toward Roger and he followed his wife through the office door.

"He's definitely up to something," Flo murmured under her breath.

"What was that, doll?"

Flo shook her head, sliding her arm through Roger's. "Nothing. Let's go have a glass of wine. I'm suddenly in dire need of one."

"Absolutely."

It was all she could do not to cast a speculative gaze toward the office door. The Newsomes were up to something and Flo needed to know what it was. She was pretty sure it had to do with the upcoming vote for the open manager's position. Which meant Flo and Agnes needed to find out who'd applied for the job.

Because whoever it was, if the Newsomes were in his or her corner, that didn't bode well for the residents of Silver Hills.

CHAPTER TWO

FLO SIPPED HER TEA and watched Agnes mop up the last of her over-easy egg yolk from her plate, with her sixth slice of toast. She'd known Agnes for several years and she didn't think she'd ever get past watching her eat. To Agnes, food was a passion. But it went beyond that, into the realm of addiction. Although, her friend approached the whole thing with such happy enthusiasm it was hard to see it as a negative.

Flo figured Agnes' doctor might disagree. "How's your blood pressure?" she asked her friend.

Agnes popped the yolk-covered chunk of toast into her mouth and smiled as she chewed. In that moment Flo realized her mistake. It was a monumental one, sure to coat everyone within a five-foot radius in chewed food.

Her hand shot up as Agnes began to open her mouth and she shook her head. "Don't! I can wait until you swallow."

Agnes' smile widened and Flo realized she'd been had. A moment later Roger strode up to the table and stopped beside Flo's chair. He placed a large hand on her shoulder, giving it a gentle squeeze. "Good morning, doll. How are you today?"

She patted his hand, smiling up at him. "I'm wonderful. How are you?"

Roger slipped into the chair next to hers and turned his coffee cup over. "A bit stiff from yesterday's yoga class." He grimaced. "I'm not too proud to admit I've underestimated yoga over the years. It's not as easy as it looks."

"The understatement of the decade," Agnes said as she wiped her lips. "I think TC's trying to kill us all. I counted the push-ups and they've doubled since last week." She shook her head. "And don't tell me they're just yoga push-ups because as far as I can tell they're just as horrible as the regular ones."

"I can't disagree," Flo told her. "I really struggle with those."

Roger looked up as their waitress approached with a steaming pot of coffee. "Morning, Becky. You're looking lovely today."

The young woman flushed with pleasure as she filled his cup. "Thank you, Mr. Attles. That's so nice of you to say."

He shrugged. "I speak only the truth."

She sighed, placing the pot on the table and cocking one hip. "I wish others were more like you. You always make my day."

He frowned, always one to take up for the underdog. "Has someone been mean to you, dear?"

Becky straightened suddenly, her face filled with alarm. "No. Of course not. I'm just making noise." She forced a smile. "Would you like the usual?"

"Not today, dear." He patted his flat belly. "I'm watching my weight. I'll just take a bowl of oatmeal, with extra raisins, and a short orange juice."

"You got it."

He watched the waitress hurry toward the kitchen, his gaze speculative.

"Roger?"

"Hm? Oh, I'm sorry doll. I was wool-gathering." He sighed. "I'm afraid I have something on my mind."

"Want to talk about it?"

"No. Oh, well, maybe. It's just that I bumped up against our charm-challenged night manager last night."

Flo and Agnes shared a look. Flo leaned close, lowering her voice. "He didn't threaten you, did he?"

"Not at all. Quite the contrary, actually. He was..." Roger frowned, settling his mug back into its saucer. "I'm not sure how to describe it. It was very disconcerting."

"Nice to you?" Flo widened her gaze as Roger looked her way.

"Yes. He was. What do you make of that?"

"Maybe he's dying," Agnes offered helpfully.

"Agnes!"

Her friend shrugged. "It would explain why he's suddenly so interested in...peopling."

"Yes," Roger said, nodding. "I'll admit that thought crossed my mind too."

"I think it's more devious than that," Flo told her friends. "I think he and Morty are lobbying for the weekend manager's position."

Agnes's mouth fell open. Thankfully it was empty. "Why would they do that? They already have manager jobs."

"Maybe they need the extra money," Flo offered. She sipped her tea and grimaced. It was cold. Happily, young Becky was striding toward them with Roger's breakfast.

"Hey you, girl! How long am I going to have to wait for my toast?"

Flo and Co turned to the table three down from theirs, where Old Mrs. Peoples sat perusing the hapless waitress looking like she'd imbibed a vinegar cocktail. The cranky nonagenarian was always unpleasant, but she looked even more sour than usual.

Becky skidded to a stop, seemed to brace herself, and then smiled as she turned. "I'm sorry, Mrs. Peoples. I didn't hear you order toast. I'll get that for you right away."

The old woman sat up straight, shoving her bony shoulders back as she feigned an alarm much more heavily weighted than the supposed crime deserved. Her wrinkled lips formed into a horrified circle. "You haven't even started making it yet? Good Heavens girl, I'm ninety-five years old. I could drop dead any minute. You want me to die without toast?"

Becky chewed on her bottom lip as her pretty brown eyes filled with tears.

Flo felt rather than saw Roger puff up with indignation and knew Old Mrs. Peoples was in for it. She turned to him. "Maybe you could wait to speak to her until after breakfast. You know there's going to be a scene."

Roger stood up and threw down his napkin.

"Or maybe not," Flo murmured.

He walked around the table and over to the young waitress, gently extracting the tray from her hands. "You go on, dear. I can take this the rest of the way."

Becky nodded, silvery tears sliding down her rosy cheeks.

Everyone in the room turned to Mrs. Peoples and frowned. The old woman was too caught up in her own indignation to notice. She shook her head and slammed the knife she'd been holding, apparently in expectation of her toast, onto the surface of the table.

Roger settled back into his seat and emptied the tray, setting it off to the side. He was very quiet.

Flo patted his hand. "It'll be okay, hun."

"No. It actually won't, doll. This is why Silver Hills is having trouble keeping wait staff. Some of the older residents are just so nasty."

Flo sighed. She knew he was right. But she was pretty sure it wasn't much better in any wait staff position. It was just a thankless type of job.

"Management should require the old cranks to eat in their apartments," Agnes said on a frown. She sat staring at her last piece of toast as if trying to decide whether to eat it.

"That's actually not a bad idea, Agnes," Roger said. "They could spin it as a perk, maybe even give them a few bucks off at the end of the month for it," Roger nodded.

"You're right," Flo agreed. "The oldies would feel like they were getting special treatment having their food delivered to their apartments and it would save the wait staff from having to endure their tantrums."

Agnes nodded.

"See, this is why I think you should put your name in for the weekend manager's job, Agnes. You'd be good at it."

To Flo's surprise, Agnes seemed to be considering it. She finally nodded. "You're right."

"I am?" Flo scanned Roger a shocked look and he grinned, scooping up a spoonful of oatmeal.

"Yes, you are. I've been thinking about it and I do think I'd do a good job." She stood up. "I'll go grab an application right now."

"I don't think Richard's in there. I saw him leave a few minutes ago, Roger told them."

Flo caught Agnes' eye and let her gaze widen just slightly. "It's okay. I was just in there. The folder is sitting on Morty's desk. I'm sure Agnes can just grab an application. Richard was very clear that he wanted her to apply."

Roger's handsome face formed into a cynical expression. "What are you up to, doll?"

Flo leaned down and kissed him on the cheek. "I'll see you later?"

He shook his head. "Of course. Stay out of trouble you two."

"Trouble is my last name. Well, it used to be. Before I had it changed." Agnes told him as they headed out of the dining room.

"I think you mean middle name," Flo told her.

"Don't be silly, Flo. My middle name is Patricia."

Flo opened her mouth to argue and then slammed it shut. There was no point. Agnes had her own way of looking at things and she was rarely dissuaded once she settled on a thought.

Agnes pulled the office door open and peered inside. "Coast is clear." She ducked inside just as a scream erupted from the dining room. Flo turned to find Old Mrs. Peoples on her feet and Tolstoy, Agnes' grim reaper cat, running away with a piece of toast clutched in his deadly jaws.

She grinned. *Karma, thy name is Tolstoy.*

By the time Flo closed the door behind her, Agnes was sitting at Morty's desk with the folder open in front of her. She'd pulled out a pile of applications and was running through them. "They've got like thirty applications here," she told Flo on a frown. "There's no way I'll get picked."

"That's not true." Flo moved around the desk and started reading over Agnes' shoulder. "These all have giant red Xs on them." It was true. Every application bore a large X on the front. "They've all been rejected."

Flo's observation didn't seem to make Agnes feel any better. Her friend had dropped her chin in her hands and was staring despondently at the contents of the folder. "Yeah, but the fox is guarding the hen house."

"Don't forget the Newsomes won't be the ones to make the decision." She blinked when Agnes frowned up at her. "Well, not the whole decision. Richard has a vote and the two finalists will go up for a resident vote."

"But who picks the finalists?" Agnes asked with a lift of one eyebrow.

Her friend had a good point. While Flo struggled to come up with a positive response, the door handle started to turn. She quickly reached down and stuffed the pages back inside the folder, slamming it shut. Agnes surged to her feet, sending the chair slamming back against the credenza behind it.

They were scurrying out from behind the desk when a blonde head poked through the crack and a pretty blue gaze was suddenly focused on them. "Oh. Hello." The young woman slipped through the door, closing it quietly behind her. She stood with her hands folded together and her gaze skittering nervously around the office. "I'm looking for Richard Attles."

Flo smiled at the woman, walking across the office. "He's stepped out for a minute, hun. Maybe we can help you? I'm Flo and this is Agnes."

The woman accepted Flo's offered hand. "Melody Tyne. It's a pleasure to meet you."

"Are you moving into Silver Hills?" Agnes asked as she pumped the delicate hand a couple of times and then dropped it.

"No. Well, probably not. Is that required?"

Flo was at a loss how to respond. "I don't think..." She skimmed a look toward Agnes.

Her friend grinned. "As far as I know there are no laws requiring people to live here." She shook her large head. "But there are worse places to live."

The woman looked back and forth between them and then gave them a confused smile. "Okay. Well. Should I wait outside?"

"For what?" Flo asked, thoroughly confused.

"For Mr. Attles?"

"If you'll tell us what you need from him, maybe we can help you."

The woman chewed her bottom lip nervously and alarm bells went off in Flo's head. Something was going on and Flo was pretty sure she wasn't going to like it. "Is everything okay, hun?"

"Yes." She gave them a nervous laugh. "I'm sorry to be so mysterious. I just wasn't sure if I should talk about it."

Flo cocked her head. Agnes frowned. A few beats later Melody Tyne sighed. "I was told to come here to discuss the vote."

Flo's spidey senses did a chicken dance through her stomach. "Vote?"

"For weekend manager. I was informed a little while ago that I was a finalist."

CHAPTER THREE

ALL THE AIR WHOOSHED out of Agnes' round belly. She sagged downward and Flo reached out to grab her arm. "You have? Congratulations, hun. Who told you that you won?"

"I received an email from Mr. Attles, just an hour ago." The young woman frowned. "Is there a problem?"

Flo slipped an arm through Agnes' and fixed her with a look, letting her eyes widen with meaning. "Not at all. We're just surprised because Agnes here is also a finalist."

Agnes swallowed hard, her eyes turning to saucers. "I am?"

Flo gave a dismissive little laugh, surreptitiously pinching Agnes.

"Ow!"

"Oh. That's wonderful." Melody Tyne told them, her tight smile telling Flo she believed it was anything but. "I guess we'll be going up against one another in the vote then."

Agnes frowned down at Flo. "Um. Yep. Looks that way."

"Well, we need to get going," Flo told the other woman. "Agnes has some glad-handing to do."

"Of course. Should I wait in here?"

Flo skimmed the tumbled folder on the desk a quick look. "Maybe you should wait in the lobby. I'm sure Mr. Attles will be back soon."

Melody nodded and left, her shoulders stiff with emotion.

As soon as she was through the door, Agnes turned to Flo. "Have you lost your tiny little mind?"

Flo scurried over and opened the file again, quickly skimming through and extracting a blank application. She folded the app in half and slipped it under her cardigan, holding it in place with her arm. "I'm pretty sure that young woman's name is not on any of those applications, Agnes."

"Maybe they pulled it because she was a finalist."

Flo hurried toward the door. "Maybe. But either way, you need to get your application to Richard right away so he can name you as the other finalist."

"But what if he doesn't think I'm qualified?" Agnes held the door as Flo slipped quickly through.

"He as much as told me you were his pick. We just need to make sure he has your application in hand so the Newsomes can't steamroll you."

Flo gave Melody Tyne a quick smile and a finger wave as they scooted past her, toward the stairs. "You can fill this out in my apartment. I need to take Rodney for a walk anyway."

The overhead lights flickered and Flo stopped in the middle of the staircase and turned toward the door. The glass entry door was already snicking shut and Vlad was walking away from it. The strange thing was, he was walking back toward the parking lot, his usual gliding stride choppy and quick.

Melody Tyne's gaze was turned upward, where the flickering lights were followed by the static in the overhead speakers that usually preceded Vlad's appearance anywhere. The younger woman was frowning.

"Flo?"

She blinked, turning back to Agnes. "What just happened down there?"

"Vlad turned tail and ran?"

"Exactly." Flo started up the steps again. "This just keeps getting weirder and weirder."

Falling in beside her, Agnes shook her wide shoulders. "Maybe it wasn't what it looked like. Maybe he just forgot something in the car."

"Maybe." But Flo didn't believe it for a minute. If she'd had any doubts before that Vlad was up to no good, she no longer did.

"There's Richard."

Flo turned as a door clicked shut up ahead. The Silver Hills day manager had just exited the therapy room and he was grinning. His smile died as Agnes called out to him, her steps hurrying closer.

Richard skimmed a quick glance toward the Emergency Exit down the hall but he must have decided he couldn't make it before Agnes overcame him. Squaring his shoulders, he pinned an insincere smile on his face and nodded. "Ladies. How are you today?"

Agnes blew his way like a level five hurricane, her eyes sparking with interest. She'd had a long-time crush on Richard that she generally managed to keep at a low boil. But every once in a while, usually when she hadn't seen him for a while, her interest bubbled over a bit, scaring everyone in the general vicinity. "I'm wonderful, Richard. Thanks so much for asking." She stopped beside him and wrapped a thick arm around his shoulders. "I was just going to fill out my application for the weekend manager's job."

He blinked, trying to step away. "Oh. That's good. I'm glad to hear it."

Agnes sighed happily.

Flo tried to signal with her eyes for Agnes to tread carefully. The last thing they wanted was for her friend to scare Richard off. They needed his help getting Agnes the position. "We just met the first finalist in your office."

"First...finalist?" Richard shook his head, clearly confused.

"Yes. Melody Tyne? She said you emailed her that she was a finalist."

Richard looked from Flo to Agnes and back again. "I don't think..."

"Fortunately for us, Agnes will win the vote. I think the residents here will respond better to someone they know and like."

"Yes, I agree but..."

"I'm so grateful for your support," Agnes gushed while making cow eyes at him.

"I..." Richard stepped firmly away, shaking his head. "I have to admit I'm at a loss, ladies. I haven't followed anything you've said since you walked over here."

Flo's spidey senses flared again. "You didn't email Melody Tyne?"

"No. At least I don't remember that name. I don't think it was in the stack of applications I went through."

Flo gave Agnes an "I told you so" look. "That's strange. Maybe Morty or Vlad contacted her and she got confused."

"Maybe." He started toward the stairs. "Is she still here?"

"Yes. We asked her to wait in the lobby."

"Good. I'll go speak with her."

"I'll have this application to you within the hour," Agnes said, her eyes still sparkling as she gazed at him.

"Okay. That would be...um...good. Thanks."

He hurried away and jogged down the steps to the lobby. Flo was pretty sure she'd never seen him move so fast before. "You laid it on a little thick, don't you think?"

Agnes shrugged. "I appreciate his help getting the job."

"Well, dial it back a bit, will you? I'm afraid you'll scare him off. Without his help Vlad and Morty will make sure you're not even considered."

"I think he's starting to like me a little bit."

Flo kept her gaze deliberately from Agnes' as they hurried down the hallway to Flo's place. Agnes and Richard Attles couldn't be further apart in terms of almost every personality trait one could measure them by. They were polar opposites. Not to mention Agnes was ten years older than Richard. But Flo just couldn't bring herself to break her friend's heart by telling her that. So she did the only thing she could. She changed the subject. "What do you suppose is going on with young Miss Tyne?"

"Like you've been saying, Vlad's up to something. He must have sent her that email as Richard."

Flo turned the key and shoved her door open. It wouldn't be hard for Vlad to do since he and Richard shared a computer. "Unless Richard's lying to us, that's the only thing that makes sense."

Flo dropped her keys onto the table in her tiny entrance-way and called out to her dog. A long, drawn-out yawn emerged from the direction of her bedroom.

"Richard wouldn't lie to us."

Flo turned to find Agnes glaring down at her. Too late, she realized how her offhand remark, meant mostly in jest, must have sounded to Agnes. In that moment Flo got a brief mental flash of their own differences, mostly physical. Where Flo was small and wiry at five feet three inches, Agnes stood nearly six feet tall and had an ex-weight lifter's build, because that was exactly what her friend was. Agnes had been one of the first professional female lifters in the United States and, at fifty-seven years old, she still lifted weights as part of her daily fitness regime. Sadly, her bulk had mostly transformed over the years into...erm...softer tissue than muscle.

Her rabid love of anything sweet and doughy hadn't helped.

"I was just kidding, fool," Flo told her friend. "You know I love and respect Richard. After all..." she smiled, "I *am* dating his father."

Agnes' broad shoulders relaxed as some of the tension left her big body. "I know that. I'm just feeling a little insecure right now, I guess."

Flo patted her arm. "Don't stress this job thing, hun. You're going to get it. We just need to stay on top of the gruesome twosome to make sure they don't pull any more fast ones."

"What about that Melody chick? She's going to be tough competition."

Flo frowned. Her friend wasn't wrong. Though Agnes had the deep inside track, Melody Tyne was young, attractive and had a feminine demeanor that would appeal to the men in the residence. "We need to find a skeleton in her closet."

Agnes' bushy, gray-brown eyebrows peaked. "Dirty politics? Why Flo, I didn't think you had it in you."

She grimaced. "Not dirty...exactly. Just slightly sullied. I'm sure she's got an unpaid parking ticket or something out there that we can use against her."

"But how are we going to find out?"

Flo gave her friend a sly look. "You forget, tomorrow is our day in the Silver City PD dungeon."

CHAPTER FOUR

A SERIES OF THUMPS above Flo's head had her frowning as she quickly perused the screen in front of her. It was a standard Internet search of Miss Melody Tyne, because Flo had quickly realized upon arriving that morning she didn't have the password needed to get into the Silver City Police Department protected database. What she'd been able to discover so far was interesting but she wasn't sure if it helped. The woman's family had apparently been involved in political activism for some time, her uncle being one of the largest bundlers of campaign cash in Indiana. There was even an article linking her uncle to Mayor Richardson, Silver City's current mayor, who would soon be stepping down. But Flo didn't see anything that linked her to Vladwick Newsome. Or explain why he might have offered her the job of Weekend Manager on the one hand, and worked to avoid her on the other.

The door at the top of the evidence dungeon stairs slammed closed and heavy footsteps pounded slowly downward.

Flo lifted her head, glancing toward the spot at the bottom where the stairwell curved to open up into the room. A dingy and scarred wall hid the person descending from view until she made that turn. "I hope you brought coffee!"

She typed Vlad's and Melody's names into the search bar, separating them with a comma, and hit search again. There had to be some connection between the two of them, somewhere.

After a moment she realized Agnes hadn't answered. She spun on her tall stool. "Agnes?"

The footsteps clomped down a few more stairs, followed by the sound of loud, wet panting. Flo was pretty sure she'd heard that sound in an emergency room before. The patient didn't last long. She jumped down off her stool and hurried over to the stairs, climbing the last four steps and taking the turn just as the massive human being on the stair above jerked to a halt to avoid hitting her.

Meany Meldick glared down at her, his wide, greasy face folded into its customary frown.

"Oh. Sorry, Officer Meldick. I thought you were Agnes."

He pulled air into his lungs and expelled it, one beefy hand flat against the wall nearest him. The wall appeared to be holding him up while he gasped for air. At 600, hairy, greasy pounds and a foul attitude, it was a safe bet Jason Meldick wouldn't be gracing any PD recruitment posters any time soon.

"Are you all right?"

He scraped sweat off his wide forehead with a beefy arm that was thick with dark brown hair. His lips parted and a dense, burgundy tongue snaked out to lick them. "I'm fine. Why does everybody keep asking me that?"

Flo lifted a brow but didn't respond verbally. If the man was truly that ignorant of his poor physical condition, nothing she said to him would make a difference.

Especially when she and Agnes had a part in keeping him that way by bribing him with pastries whenever they needed information. "She left a while ago to get some donuts. Did you see her?"

Meldick flicked a hand in her direction and started moving again as Flo retreated back down the steps. He didn't even try to talk until his size thirteen feet rested on the dirty concrete. Flo chewed her bottom lip. If coming down the steps had made him nearly need an oxygen tank, she couldn't even imagine what going back up would do.

She moved across the room, picking up a large evidence bag with a coiled, leather whip inside. She didn't even want to know what that was about. "I was just cataloging some things."

He grunted wetly and started shuffling in her direction.

Flo flicked the screen a quick glance, realizing she hadn't shut down the browser. "And, erm, doing a little research."

Officer Meldick groaned heavily as he lowered himself to the stool. He scraped another layer of sweat off his brow with his uniform sleeve and spun around. "Agnes already filled me in. She bribed me with chocolate croissants from Moe's if I help."

Flo grinned. Everybody wanted a food motivated pet. They were so much easier to train. "Great! That explains why she's not back yet." Moe's was clear across town and, on a Saturday morning the city's most popular bakery would be packed.

Hopefully Agnes wouldn't eat all of Meanie's croissants before she got back.

"Did she tell you what we needed?"

He placed fingers the size of small baguettes on the keyboard and started typing. "Background on a private citizen."

He stopped typing and gave Flo the eye. "I'm not sharing anything intensely personal on this woman."

Flo nodded. "I wouldn't want to intrude on her privacy. I just want to know about anything that's in the public arena."

"Like what?" He asked, sniffing loudly.

"Lawsuits, tickets, charges of any kind."

"Against her or from her?"

Flo shrugged. "Both I guess. I'm trying to figure out how this woman went straight to the head of the line at Silver Hills."

Meldick tapped a few keys and perused the screen.

Flo moved closer and he turned to glare at her. "Stay back, Mrs. Bee. No reading over my shoulder."

She lifted her hands in surrender.

The door at the top of the steps slammed and footsteps moved quickly and heavily down the staircase. "Hello?"

"Down here, Agnes," Flo called out. She watched Meldick carefully, hoping he'd look away long enough for her to sneak a peek at the screen. But the man was like a bulldog with a chicken flavored rawhide. He wasn't going to let Flo anywhere near whatever he might find.

"I bought a dozen chocolate croissants," Agnes announced as she entered the dungeon. She carried a large, grease spotted box perched on top of one hand, her other hand holding a carrier with three cups of coffee in it. She handed the carrier to Flo and settled the box onto the table next to the computer.

Meldick's greasy nose twitched but he didn't turn to look. "How many are left," he asked Agnes, fingers still tapping away.

She gave him fake outrage which he didn't bother to notice and then winked at Flo. "I left you a couple."

He shook his buffalo sized head. "Good thing I had a late breakfast."

"Have you found anything interesting?" Agnes moved in behind him, trying to peer over his shoulder. He promptly reached over and shut the monitor off.

"Hey!"

The cranky cop reached into the box, pulling out a massive croissant filled with chocolate. "No peeking."

They waited while he stuffed the pastry into his mouth and chewed, taking his time eating the first of the three Agnes had left in the box.

Flo sipped her coffee and waited impatiently, her fingers drumming on top of the long table filled with evidence.

Meldick finally arched a shaggy brow at her. "Don't you have work to do?"

She did. Unluckily. But she wasn't interested in cataloging evidence when there was a possible mystery going on at Silver Hills. "I need the computer." It was a partial truth. There was filing she could do. But she wasn't going to tell him that. If she kept staring at him, maybe he'd give up the stall tactics and help a sistah out.

Meldick chewed slowly, like a cow with his cud, and reached a pudgy mitt toward the last croissant in the box.

Flo struggled with the urge to yank that whip out of its bag and put it to good use.

Meldick's radio crackled and he reached down, turning the volume up as he placed the last bite of his second breakfast back in the box.

The 911 operator's voice came on line, sounding tinny and broken because of poor reception in the basement area.

Available units reply to a 10-54 at 1125 Miller Ave.

Meldick flinched, swallowed the bite of pastry in his mouth, and squinted at the screen.

"What's wrong?" Flo tried to move closer to see what he was looking at but Meanie Meldick closed out of the database and struggled to his feet with a groan. "Gotta go, ladies."

"But you promised to help us," Agnes said.

He reached out and grabbed what was left of the croissant. "And I will, three measly croissants worth. Don't worry about that lady you asked about. She's not gonna get Agnes' manager job." He stuffed the pastry into his mouth and lumbered toward the stairs.

Flo glared after him, wishing she'd used the whip. "What does that mean?"

He threw a crumb-coated smile her way and waved as he wrenched his big foot up onto the first step.

Agnes flopped down on the computer stool with a sigh. "Sorry, Flo. I shouldn't have eaten all those croissants."

Flo frowned, watching Meldick's big boohind disappear up the stairs. Something was wrong. She slid her gaze to the darkened computer screen. He'd been scanning the database...seemingly finding nothing to alarm...when the radio call went out.

Realization struck. "That's it!" Flo started toward the stairs, hitting the bottom one as Meldick slammed the door at the top.

"Wait, Flo. Where are you going?"

"To talk to Selma."

Agnes fell in behind her. "The 911 operator? Why?"

"Because I think that call we heard involved Melody Tyne."

"The 10-4?"

"It was 10 something. And unless I'm really off the mark, I'm guessing whatever that code was, it wasn't good news for your rival."

"POSSIBLE DEAD BODY," the woman sitting behind the computer in a small, darkened room on the main level told them. She narrowed watery hazel eyes at Flo, her wrinkled lips pursing. "Why do you ask?"

"We think it had to do with a friend of ours?"

Selma grabbed her mouse and used the wheel to scroll up her screen. She squinted at the series of fields there, her deft finger moving the cursor over the provided information so quickly Flo had trouble following. But she did spot the address bar and quickly committed it to memory.

Selma suddenly seemed to realize she was giving personal information to a civilian and she turned in her chair, blocking the screen with her well-padded body. "Can you give me this person's name?"

"Melody Tyne," Flo offered as Agnes slipped around Selma's chair trying for a look.

The older woman had been a 911 operator with the Silver City PD for twenty years. She knew all the tricks.

She swung around and fixed a hostile gaze on Agnes. "Step away, Agnes."

Agnes lifted her hands, stepping back. To Flo's surprise she had a small, white bag clutched in one of them. "I was just going to put this on your desk."

Flo made a mental note to ask her friend where she'd been hiding that bag.

Selma reached for the bag as if it might have a snake inside. "What is it?"

"A chocolate croissant from Moe's."

Selma's watery gaze widened with pleasure. "You don't say!"

"I do say," Agnes told her with a grin. "I brought a whole box of them back with me. I wanted to make sure you got one."

"Well isn't that sweet." She shook her head, the rat's nest of soft gray curls barely moving. "Thanks, honey."

"My pleasure."

"Selma, I know we're asking you to give us private information. I don't need the address or anything. We just wondered if Melody Tyne was the possible dead body?"

Selma pursed her lips. "I'm sorry, Flo. I can't tell you that. The patrol cars haven't gotten to the scene yet. All I can tell you is that the house belongs to an M. Tyne."

"Okay." Flo reached out and clasped Selma's hand, giving it a squeeze. "Enjoy your croissant, hun."

"Oh, I will." She turned back to her screen and settled the bag onto her desk as she pulled it open and stuck her nose inside.

Flo gave the flat spot on the back of the woman's head a final look before turning around and trying not to run out of the room.

Agnes showed unusual restraint by not asking any questions until they were outside the building. "Okay, slow up and tell me what's going on."

Flo kept moving. "I think Melody Tyne's been killed."

"Killed? That sweet young thing?"

Flo yanked her car door open. "That sweet young thing who was awarded a finalist's position for the manager's job without anybody seeming to know her? The same sweet young woman whom Vlad seems to be avoiding like the plague? I told you something wasn't right about that. And now she might be dead."

Agnes stood where she was as Flo slid behind the wheel. Finally, she turned around. "Are you coming or not?"

"Where?" Agnes asked with more than a little frustration coloring her voice.

"To Melody Tyne's home. I want to see if she's dead and if the police know anything about how she died."

Agnes shook her head. But she moved around the car and slid inside with a soft crackling noise. "We don't even know where she lives."

Flo grinned as she started the car and put it in reverse. "I know. But what I don't know is where that bag came from that you gave Selma."

Agnes chuckled. "Stuffed in the waistband of my pants. Which reminds me…" She reached under her shirt and, amid more crackling sounds, came up with another bag. "Want a croissant?"

"Good heavens, no!"

CHAPTER FIVE

THE ADDRESS THEY WERE looking for was clear on the other end of Silver City, in a part of the city where Flo, fortunately didn't spend much time.

"Ugh, this is awful," Agnes groaned. She sat with her nose practically pressed against the window, her lips pursed with disgust. "Do you think she really lives here?"

Flo pulled into a small, gravel parking lot that was covered in weeds and other things best not examined too closely. The building squatting next to the lot had clearly seen better days, and too many rough nights. Flo stared at the two squad cars sitting crookedly across the space directly in front of the sidewalk, wondering who they'd sent to the scene.

"I hope it's Ginger and Robald," Agnes said. "They owe me ten dollars each from that last poker game."

Flo shook her head. "I made them pay me the hundred they owed me right away. I don't trust them to pay up once they leave the table."

Agnes narrowed her gaze on Flo. "That's a lot of money. It's not fair to use your harmless old lady ways to lure victims into poker games. People look at you and think you'd lose at *Go*

Fish just to keep from hurting somebody's feelings. They have no idea they're being stalked by a card shark."

Flo tried to look innocent. "I have no idea what you're talking about. I wanted to play Monopoly but they insisted." She pressed her lips together to stop the grin dancing there. It was true people looked at her tiny stature, rosy cheeks and soft bouff dressed in the color of the week and assumed she was harmless. But that wasn't her fault. She never actively set out to fool anybody. Well...not that often anyway. "You know Mr. Bee and I used to host monthly poker parties when he was alive. We took our poker very seriously."

Agnes snorted. "Jeffry Dommer took his man-made brisket seriously. What you do is more like a religion."

Flo rolled her eyes.

"Oh, oh."

"What's wrong?"

"Well, the good news is that Ginger and Robald are here."

Flo reached for the door handle.

"But the bad news is that they're not alone."

Three people were walking down the sidewalk, toward the squad cars. Behind them, two EMTs pushed a gurney carrying a black body bag toward the waiting ambulance. She couldn't see enough of the threesome behind the cars to recognize them. Flo nearly groaned. "Please don't tell me Brent Peters is the Detective in charge?"

"Nope. It's worse than that."

Flo craned her neck, lifting off the seat to try to see who it was. She needn't have bothered. The shortish, strongly made woman with the red hair that inspired her nickname walked around her squad car and climbed in behind the wheel. The other uniformed cop waved at the third person and climbed into the car too, barely getting his door closed before Ginger quickly backed the squad car away from the curb and tore off, lights and sirens flaring.

That left only one squad car and the space between Flo and the waiting cop free.

"Satan's boogers," Flo breathed. "Not Nightshade."

Beside her, Agnes sighed.

They climbed out of Flo's car and started toward him. Flo could only hope the handsome detective had forgiven Agnes for assaulting him the last time they'd worked together. But judging by his cool demeanor every time he passed them in the halls of the Silver City PD, Flo doubted it.

He stood on the sidewalk, tall and strongly built, with white-blond hair that he wore slicked straight back. His blue eyes flashed with automatic irritation when he saw them and his movie star jaw tensed. Flo could almost hear his perfect white teeth grinding together as they approached.

She forced a smile she knew would be rejected. "Detective Nightshade. Fancy meeting you here."

He narrowed his cool gaze. "Yes. It's quite a surprise. I suppose you're heading inside to debauch the crime scene?"

Flo's chuckle sounded strained, even to her. "You're such a jokester."

He lifted a well-shaped blond eyebrow.

"We're here to see if Miss Tyne's all right."

The other brow lifted to join the first one. "I wasn't aware you knew Ms. Tyne."

"Oh yes, we met her at Silver Hills. Such a nice young woman."

"We couldn't believe it when we heard she was dead," Agnes blurted.

Nightshade's hostile blue gaze swung her way. "Oh really? And how exactly did you hear that?"

Flo wanted to pinch Agnes's head off. Instead she coughed loudly, smacking Agnes on the hip as she did.

"Ow!"

Flo glared her way. "We just assumed it, I'm afraid. When we heard the code and her address. Is it true? Is young Miss Tyne dead?"

Nightshade gave them a long look and a slow smile, and then strode past them, to the two-door sports car parked under a tree at the far corner of the small lot. "Stay away from that crime scene, ladies," he told them as he slipped inside.

Flo eagerly watched him as he started the car and pulled slowly past, a smug grin on his too-handsome face.

"Such a jerk," Agnes said.

Flo nodded. "I don't like the way he was grinning at us. What do you suppose it meant?"

"He's probably going to drive around the block and come back to catch us checking out the crime scene."

"Could be." Flo stared thoughtfully down the road, where Nightshade's brake lights blinked once before he took the turn and sped away.

"Are we going in?"

Behind them, a door slammed closed and they turned to find a uniformed cop standing on the stoop. He lifted his chin when he saw them looking his way. "Ladies. Did Detective Nightshade send you over with more tape?"

Recognizing young Nicholas Bachus, Flo grinned. At only twenty-five, Bachus was still young enough to respect his elders, and new enough that he didn't realize he couldn't trust them. "Hello, Nick. He did. But I'm afraid Agnes forgot to grab it before we left."

The boy's brown eyes narrowed on Agnes and then he grinned. "Way to go, Agnes."

She shrugged, grinning comically. "What can I say, I had a senior moment."

Bachus laughed, shaking his head. He pulled a cigarette out of the pack in his pocket and lit it up, drawing deeply.

Flo frowned. "You should stop smoking, hun. That's really bad for you."

He took another long drag and expelled it to the side, away from Flo and Agnes. "I know, ma'am. But it's just so hard to quit."

"I know, hun." She gave him a soft smile. "They left you all alone here?"

Bachus nodded, smoke spiraling lazily from his nose. "The body's gone. I'm just supposed to make sure nobody disturbs the scene until the CSU guys get here."

"They haven't come yet?"

"No. Something went down across town. Four bodies found in a small apartment. They think drugs were involved." He shrugged. "Trouble with bein' a small town. There's only so much personnel to pull in when things go South."

"I hear ya," Agnes said, nodding. "What happened here?"

The kid took another drag and smiled as he exhaled. "Nice try, Agnes."

"As a favor, Nicholas? We knew the victim," Flo told him. "We just want to make sure her death isn't tied to Silver Hills."

"Why would it be tied to your place?" he asked, frowning.

"Melody Tyne was about to take a job there. That's how we know her," Agnes told the cop.

"Really?" He threw his cigarette down and ground it into the broken concrete. Then, when Flo glared at him he picked it up and dropped it into his pocket. "I'm surprised she was still up to working."

Flo felt the first flutter of unease in her belly. "Why?"

He shrugged. "I don't want to insult anybody..."

"Nicholas..." Flo warned.

He shook his head. "You don't need to see the crime scene."

Agnes heaved a sigh. "Come on, Nick."

"Nightshade told you not to let us in, didn't he?" Flo shook her head. "That man hates us."

"Well yeah," the young cop grinned widely. "But that's not why. You don't need to see it because the corpse wasn't Melody Tyne. It was her mother, Melissa Tyne. As far as I know, the daughter doesn't even live here."

"SLOW DOWN, FLO. TELL me where we're going," Agnes huffed.

Flo pulled the door open to Silver Hills and waved as someone called out a greeting from the bar. "We need to find out more about Melody Tyne. Something's going on with that girl and I want to know what."

Agnes sucked air as Flo hurried across the lobby. "But you heard Nick. She wasn't the one who died. It was her mother."

Footsteps slapped up behind them and someone called Flo's name. She suddenly realized who it was and stopped, turning.

Their friend Trisha Columbo, better known as TC around Silver Hills, jogged lightly up to them, her rubber flip flops slapping against the marble floor. She stopped a few feet away and walked toward them, not even breathing hard. In her mid-thirties, TC was also the activities director at Silver Hills and she was very fit. Her lithe, five foot six inch frame was lean and taut and her energy level seemed endless. Flo envied her that youthful energy. Her own *energy* was mostly in her mind and her body sometimes had trouble keeping up. Flo smiled at her friend. "Hi, hun. How are you?"

TC swung her gaze over her two friends. "What have you two been up to?"

"Why do you assume we're up to something?" Agnes asked defensively.

TC's eyes narrowed. "Are you breathing?"

Agnes' good humor returned and she chuckled. "Okay, you got me on that one."

Flo reached out and clasped TC's hand. "We need to use your computer, hun."

"What for?"

"Maybe I just want to order yoga pants," Agnes said with a raised brow.

TC snorted. "Yeah, right."

"We need to do some research," Flo told her, tugging TC into movement. "There's been another murder."

TC dragged to a stop, pulling her hand from Flo's grasp. "Absolutely not! Brent's just started speaking to me again after the last investigation you interfered in."

"The good news is that your boyfriend isn't involved in this investigation," Agnes told her with a grin.

"It's Detective Nightshade," Flo admitted.

"Oh," TC said, frowning thoughtfully. "You sure?"

"We spoke to him not twenty minutes ago."

TC weighed the information for a moment and then nodded. "Okay. But if Brent gets involved you have to promise me you'll back off."

"Of course, hun," Flo assured her friend. So what if she was crossing her fingers behind her back?

TC wasn't fooled. "Um hm. I just want you to know there will never be any tiny little TCs running around this world and it will all be your fault." Frowning, TC started toward her office.

"You could find another man," Agnes replied with a practicality that was unusual for her.

"But I like this one," TC whined. She stopped in front of her door and pulled out a key card, sliding it through the reader.

"Oh, that's cool," Agnes said. "I want one."

TC pushed the door open and flipped the lights on. "This is part of the new upgrades."

Flo stared at the new reader, her mind swirling. There had been a lot of upgrades lately. She wondered how *Future Group*, the owners of Silver Hills, were paying for it all. "I guess our rent's going up then?"

TC lowered herself into her chair and started punching buttons on her computer. "Not that I know of."

"Something's changed, hun," Flo argued. "First the new large screen TVs in the common rooms, then they informed us the whole place would be getting new carpet..."

"I'm glad we're getting new carpet," Agnes said, flopping into a chair across the room. "My carpet smells bad."

Flo lifted an eyebrow. "That's because the Grim Reaper pees on it all the time."

TC grimaced.

"He does not!" Agnes argued a little to emphatically.

"Me thinks thou dost protest too much," Flo told her with a triumphant grin.

"Huh?"

TC rolled her eyes. "Stop fighting children." She looked at Flo. "What are we looking for?"

Fortunately for their purposes, TC wrote murder mysteries for a second vocation, so she was better than average at researching stuff. When she suggested using TC's office computer, Flo hadn't intended for her friend to do the work on the computer, but she was starting to realize it was a very good idea.

"See what you can come up with on Melissa Tyne."

"Is that the person who was murdered?"

"Yes," Flo told her.

TC typed the name into the search bar as Flo moved to look over her shoulder. Several articles popped up and Flo scanned the excerpts quickly. Most of them were clearly about another woman. They talked about her aspirations to become an Olympic athlete. "That's not her. This woman would probably be in her sixties."

"Do you have an address?"

Flo rattled off the address they'd just visited.

A moment later they hit pay dirt. It was a long article about a local slumlord and the residents who were suing him for unsafe conditions. The picture they provided was of a woman who could have been in her late fifties or early sixties, whose features resembled the pretty young woman they'd met in the Silver Hills office. The caption under the picture confirmed Flo's suspicions. "Melissa Tyne. She was leading the class action suit against the building's landlord." She frowned. Something niggled but Flo couldn't quite put her finger on it. "Can you print that out?"

TC nodded and sent the document to her printer.

When it finished printing, Flo grabbed it and started reading from the top. From what she was seeing, the slumlord they were suing had buildings all over Silver City. Mrs. Tyne claimed he'd ignored multiple requests to fix the air conditioning in her apartment, despite the fact that temperatures the previous summer had reached a hundred plus degrees for a couple of weeks in a row. She claimed she would have expired from the heat if she hadn't moved out until the weather cooled.

The article went on to provide a laundry list of complaints from other residents including everything from backed up toilets to a leaky roof and wiring that flared and sparked. "Good heavens," she said, dropping into the chair across from TC. "That place is dangerous."

TC had been reading along and she looked concerned. "I'm glad they're suing this jerk."

"*Nightowl, Inc.*," Flo read in the article. "See what you can find on them."

TC began typing, stopping every few minutes to scan and click. Several minutes later she shook her head. "The owner's name is hidden. Whoever set this up didn't want to be found."

Flo bit her bottom lip. "Maybe we can get the information at the station."

TC laughed, clearly thinking Flo was joking. When she realized she wasn't, TC's pretty face opened into a look of astonishment. "You don't really think the detectives are going to give you that information?"

"Not on purpose, no," Flo told her.

TC closed her eyes and dropped heavily back in her chair. "I really don't like where this is going."

"Jamie!"

Flo jumped an inch off her chair and slapped a hand against her chest. "Good heavens, fool, you scared me half to death."

Agnes shrugged. "I can't believe you didn't hear me walk up behind you. I'm not exactly light on my feet."

Flo inhaled for calm. "What are you blathering on about?"

Agnes pointed to the byline which Flo had totally missed. "This was written by Jamie Poyrie."

"So it was!" Flo grinned and stood up. "I think it's time we visited Jamie at work, don't you, Agnes?"

CHAPTER SIX

FLO AND AGNES ROLLED up into the small, brown-brick building that housed the Silver City Tribune and approached the information desk. The woman behind the desk looked up at them and smiled. "Can I help you?"

"We'd like to speak to Jamie Poyrie, please," Flo told the woman.

"Let me see if Jamie's in right now." The woman tapped the comm system in front of her and spoke softly into the headphones denting her iron gray bouff. A moment later she looked up. "Jamie's in a meeting right now. If you'll have a seat she'll be out to see you in a few minutes."

Flo thanked the woman and walked over to a table covered with used newspapers from that morning.

Agnes flopped ungracefully into a chair. "I hope this doesn't take long. I'm starving."

Flo rolled her eyes. "You had a cookie on the way over here."

"One little cookie. It barely made a dent in my hunger. I'm feeling kind of faint. I think my blood sugar's crashing."

"If your blood sugar actually ever crashed, it would probably make a hole in the floor. It's less blood and more sugar."

"Har de har har, miss comedian."

"Ladies!"

They looked up to find a slim young black woman bearing down on them, her long black hair dancing around her pretty face in beaded braids.

"Oh, I love the hair!" Agnes told Jamie before accepting a hug.

"Thank you! I'm glad to hear that. My dad hates it."

Flo took her own hug and then pulled back with a smile. "You look beautiful as always. How are you doing?"

"Pretty good. They're keeping me busy." She smiled happily as she said it and Flo realized the young woman was finally hitting her stride at the paper. She certainly deserved some success after all she'd been through. "How are you two doing?"

Agnes put a hand on her round belly and opened her mouth. Flo cut her off before she could complain about being hungry. "We're fine. We were wondering if you could come out with us and get a coffee or something."

"Pie with ice cream," Agnes added, beaming.

Jamie looked at her watch, clearly considering whether she had the time. "I think I could spare a half hour." She turned and glanced at the woman behind the desk and the receptionist nodded. "Enjoy, honey."

"I wish we could go to Frankie's," Agnes lamented as they climbed into Flo's car. "He makes the best cherry pie."

Jamie grinned. "He does, doesn't he. Papa's always been a great baker."

"No time to go that far, Agnes. We'll have to go there another time."

"I happen to know the dinner special tonight is jambalaya and cheesy cornbread."

Agnes moaned with pleasure. "I'm there."

Flo shook her head. "Don't encourage her, Jamie."

The young reporter giggled. "It's my job to keep shoving people toward papa's restaurant, Mrs. Bee. You know that."

"And you do it so well, hun." Flo shared a grin with their young friend and pulled off the road, into the parking lot of a stainless steel and glass diner.

"What's up?" she asked Flo. "Not that I'm sorry you came to see me, but I know you two. You're mixed up in something aren't you?"

"I'll explain when we're seated."

True to her word, Flo waited until they were in a booth and had ordered before turning to Jamie. "We read your article about that slumlord."

Jamie sighed. "That's so sad. I knew someone was going to get hurt there."

"You're referring to Melissa Tyne?"

Jamie's eyes went round. "No. What happened to Mrs. Tyne?"

"Oh. We'll get to that. Has someone else been hurt?"

"An elderly woman at an apartment across town. Her water wasn't working for days so she just stopped drinking. They found her this morning. She died of dehydration."

"Dementia?" Flo asked softly. It wasn't uncommon for elderly people to neglect drinking enough fluids because the center of their brain that controls thirst was one of the areas that degenerated with dementia.

"I think so. Sadly, she didn't have any family looking after her. Her only son lives in Colorado. He's flying back now."

They stopped talking for a beat while the waitress settled their coffee cups and plates of pie in front of them.

Agnes picked up her fork and tucked into it, hesitating only long enough to ask Jamie the question Flo was about to ask. "How do you know so much about it?"

"I'm writing the story. It's becoming kind of an expose. This company that owns these apartments around Silver City also owns a dozen more residential buildings around the state. Each one seems almost worse than the last."

"*Nightowl, Inc.*," Flo said, wiping her lips. "We did some research with TC's help. Any idea who owns the company?"

"Not yet. It's either somebody really powerful or really motivated to stay off the radar. Every time we uncover a layer and think we're getting close we bump up against another layer." She sighed. "Frustrating." Jamie took a bite of her blueberry pie, chewing thoughtfully.

"I can imagine, hun."

She nodded, swallowing. "What happened to Melissa Tyne?"

"She's dead. But I don't think you can blame her death on *Nightowl*. We think she was murdered."

"Oh no!"

Flo nodded. "We met her daughter at Silver Hills and, when we heard the call go out on the police radio we thought it was her." Flo didn't bother explaining how they'd really discovered the body, it wasn't necessary for their conversation with Jamie.

Jamie settled her fork onto her half-eaten pie. "And you want to find out what happened to her, don't you?" Jamie's brown eyes sparkled with humor.

"Actually, we're trying to figure out if it has something to do with Silver Hills."

"Why in the world would it?" Jamie asked.

Flo took her through the meeting with Melody and her concerns about Vlad's influence. "I want to know why a man who generally can't stand people is going around glad-handing people and interfering with the search for a weekend manager."

"And why he's hiding from Melody Tyne," Agnes added.

"I agree that's a mystery, but it seems a stretch from what you're telling me."

Flo raised her brows. "You're telling me you think it's a co-incidence?"

Jamie shrugged. "It certainly could be." She picked up her fork and poked at her pie, clearly not interested in finishing it. "I can probably help. But not in the way you're expecting. It seems likely that you're wrong about *Nightowl*." She looked up, her expression earnest. "They definitely could be involved in Mrs. Tyne's murder."

"Why do you say that, hun?"

"Because Melody and Melissa Tyne were the leaders of a huge class action suit going after *Nightowl, Inc*. In fact, Mrs. Tyne had called in some favors with the Mayor and it was starting to look as if there would be a task force assigned to look into the organization."

Flo thought about that for a moment and then had a sudden, disturbing thought. "Oh my. If *Nightowl* is responsible for Mrs. Tyne's death..."

Judging by the way her eyes widened, Jamie seemed to have the same thought at the same time. "Then Melody could be next on their list."

UNLIKE HER MOTHER, Melody Tyne lived in a decent home on a decent street with small but tidy houses on large, well-tended lots. The house was set back a ways and the driveway they pulled into was lined on either side by mature trees. As Flo drove slowly toward the detached garage, located off to the side of the home, her tires crunched over walnuts and fallen tree debris. "This is a nice place," Agnes said, leaning forward to peer between Flo and Jamie at the house. "I wonder why her mom didn't live with her."

Flo parked near the sidewalk leading to the front door. "Maybe her mom didn't want to live with her. My son asked me to move in with him when I sold my house and I gave him an unequivocal *No Thanks*!"

Jamie chuckled. "I can't imagine living with pops. He'd make me absolutely crazy."

They climbed out of the car and headed toward the front door, which was painted a unique shade of bright green. Fortunately, Melody hadn't used the same neon color on the black shutters gracing the windows across the front of the white home.

A large pot of flowers dominated the small, concrete porch and an Adirondack rocking chair sat next to it. "How pretty," Flo said as she reached down to touch the flowers. "I love Petunias."

"Me too," Jamie agreed. "They come in such pretty colors."

Agnes slammed a fist on the front door and it swung open. "Oops..."

Flo gave her friend a quelling look. "You broke the door?"

"I didn't break it, Flo. It wasn't latched."

Virtual thought bubbles popped up above all their heads and Flo figured her friends' mutual look of terrified realization was mirrored on her own face. Her stomach rolled with unease. "We're too late."

Agnes plowed through the door before Flo could stop her and Jamie's eyes went wide. "You need to get her back out here. Somebody might be waiting inside."

Flo nodded. "You call the police. I'll get Agnes."

But by the time Flo got inside, Agnes had already hoofed it across the small house and was standing in an open doorway at the back, her shoulders rigid.

Flo hurried to reach her, whispering loudly. "Get out of this house, fool! If something's happened to Melody, the people who hurt her could still be in here..."

Agnes turned a pair of eyes made googly with shock toward Flo. "Oh, something's happened to Melody."

Flo barely kept from groaning as she peered around Agnes' big body. "Please don't tell me they killed her too."

Agnes shifted her weight sideways so Flo could look into the room. "Okay, but I'm pretty sure she didn't trip and land inside that belt and strangle herself."

"Flo! Agnes!" Jamie's voice carried to them from the front door, her tone urgent.

Flo stared at the horrific scene laid out before her, her throat clenching so she couldn't have spoken if she wanted to.

Melody Tyne lay sprawled over the rug next to her bed, a length of fuzzy pink belt wrapped tightly around her throat. Her once-pretty eyes bulged from a purple-hued face and her fingers dug ineffectually at what looked like the belt from a robe that someone had clearly strangled her with.

"Oh no!" Jamie's voice from directly behind Flo made her jump and turn.

"Did you call the police?"

Jamie nodded, her gaze locked on the unfortunate victim on the floor. "I can't believe they killed her too."

She wobbled unsteadily, looking for all the world as if she was going to faint. Flo grabbed her before she fell. "Lean on me, hun. Breathe deeply. You'll be all right."

Jamie shook her head, looking anything but all right. "I feel sick..."

"Oh dear." Flo glanced toward the front door. "Maybe you should go outside. Detective Nightshade won't be happy if you throw up on his crime scene."

"There's the robe the belt came from..."

Agnes' voice cut through Flo's distraction and she suddenly realized her friend was no longer in the doorway beside her. She whipped around. "No! Agnes!"

Agnes was standing next to the body, her gaze fixed on a drape of pink cloth lying in a puddle beside the bathroom door. Flo let go of Jamie and started forward. "Get out of this room right now, Agnes before you..."

But she was too late.

As Agnes took a step toward the robe, her foot caught in the murder weapon and the belt whipped around her ankle like a boa constrictor. Agnes's stride was cut short by the corpse-weighted entanglement and she yelped as she stumbled forward, dragging poor Miss Tyne's corpse several feet across the room. Agnes slammed into the woman's dresser and went down to her knees, yanking the furniture with her. She ended up sprawled on her back, knees bent uncomfortably beneath her, and the contents of the shattered dresser draped all over her head and shoulders.

She lay there for a moment, groaning as Flo hurried forward.

"Are you all right?"

Flo shoved a lace nighty off Agnes's shoulder and tried to get a grip under her arm to pull her off the floor. It was impossible. Between Agnes' weight and the weight of the dresser, Flo couldn't move her even an inch. "My goodness, Agnes. Detective Nightshade's going to kill us."

Agnes expelled air, sending a tiny slip of siren red silk and lace into the air to slide down the top of the overturned dresser until it caught on a broken drawer. A matching bra was perched over Agnes' gray brown pageboy like a pair of cat ears. "I didn't do it on purpose."

"You never do, hun." Flo tried again to extricate Agnes and then gave up, panting from the effort. "We'll need to get this dresser off you first. Jamie can you help..."

Uugh!

Flo's head snapped around.

Uugh!

"No, Jamie don't..."

Uugggghhhhhhhh, blahhhhhhhhck!

"Oh, good Lord in Heaven." Flo jumped out of the way as Jamie gave up the contents of her stomach. Depositing the remains of her blueberry pie all over Melody Tyne's corpse.

CHAPTER SEVEN

THEY STAYED AS FAR away from Detective Nightshade as they could get in the small house. Unhappily, it wasn't far enough. They could hear him muttering and swearing and trying to explain to the crime scene guys that they had to notate the change in position of the body and extra broken bones due to tampering of the scene.

Nobody was happy with that situation.

But that was happy time compared to what went down in that room when they saw Jamie's contribution to the scene.

Poor Jamie looked miserable. She wasn't used to being on the wrong side of the law...even if it was only a crime of biological trespassing. She turned a worried gaze to Flo. "Do you think they'll throw us in the clinker?"

Flo fought a smile. "The clinker? Do you mean the clink, hun?"

Jamie waved a hand. "Whatever. My boss is gonna kill me."

"Why? You're just doing investigative reporting," Flo said.

"Yeah, from the inside," Agnes added with a snort.

"This isn't funny, Agnes." Jamie's brown eyes filled with tears. "We defiled a crime scene."

Agnes shook her head. "I just defiled a dresser. You defiled a corpse."

"Not helping, fool," Flo muttered as Jamie's lip started to quiver. "Don't worry, hun. I'll talk to Nightshade."

"What are you going to talk to me about?" a deep voice asked from across the room.

They turned to find the Detective striding their way, his handsome face a mask of rage. "I hope you don't think you're going to be able to talk your way out of this one, Bee. You've gone too far this time."

Flo blanched. He'd resorted to calling her by her last name. That didn't bode well for a positive outcome. "Now look, Detective..."

"Stop talking." He held up a big hand, still covered in puke-painted latex.

Before she could stop herself, Flo grimaced.

He noticed and quickly realized the reason. "Ugh!" Nightshade grabbed the edge of the glove with the tippy tips of his blunt edged fingers and peeled it off, flinging it aside. "You'll be doing dungeon duty for a decade if I have anything to say about it."

Flo tried to frown. He was mistaken if he thought that would be a punishment. She actually enjoyed being at the police station. It made her burgeoning detective career much easier to manage. But she didn't want him to know that. If he did he'd do everything he could to ruin it for her. "You wouldn't dare."

He bent closer, his lips twisting with disgust. "Try me."

Flo shook her head. "We didn't come here planning to mess up your scene, Detective. We came with the hope of saving Melody Tyne's life."

He pressed his lips into a tight, thin line and made a sound that was dangerously close to a growl. "It's too bad she wasn't still alive when you got here. She might have been able to defend herself against you three."

"That's just mean," Agnes said, frowning. "Take it back or I'll punch you again."

Flo moved quickly to get in between them. The last time Agnes had punched Nightshade they'd thought he was a criminal. Or at the very least a devil worshiper. But they no longer had that excuse. They knew he was a cop and Flo doubted he'd let Agnes walk away from punching him again.

Besides, it had to be hard on his ego to have been bested by a girl. Even if that girl was over two hundred pounds of attitude and muscle...well there had to be some muscle in there, Flo decided.

"Take your best shot, Willard."

"You're still a bully, Nightshade," Agnes huffed. "And you know what I do to bullies."

"Oookkay," Flo said. "We're all last names now."

Nightshade put his hand on the cuffs dangling from the pocket of his jeans. "You wanna try? I'll have you cuffed and in jail before you can say 'I'm an idiot.'"

"You're an idiot," Agnes told him, grinning. "I guess you're not as fast as you think you are."

Nightshade lunged.

Agnes clenched her fists and stepped toward him, clearly not smart enough to know when to back down.

Flo found herself sandwiched painfully between them, her face smushed into Nightshade's jacket. "Mmff mef bmff bfe!" she lifted her arms, flailing to get their attention. When that didn't work she tried shoving Nightshade away. He didn't budge an inch.

They ignored her, stepping even closer to one another. Agnes lifted a fist and Flo swung at it, trying to fling her friend's arm off course before it connected with the cop. She could barely see the arm with her face smashed into his jacket and she missed badly, whacking Nightshade on a jean-clad hip. He growled, his chest rumbling under Flo's nose.

"Fmfe blmff!" Flo tried to shove him away but didn't have any better success than before.

"Stop it you two!" Jamie's voice was pitched high with concern. The strident tone must have cut through the red haze the two combatants appeared to be mired in. They stopped suddenly. "Step back you two! You're smothering poor Flo." A soft hand with long, slender fingers found her wrist, tugging gently as Nightshade and Agnes eased apart.

"You okay, Mrs. Bee? They dented your hair and everything." Jamie's hand hovered over Flo's bouff as if she wanted to put it back to rights. Flo stepped neatly aside, lifting her own hand to re-pouf the bouff.

"I'm fine, hun." Flo glared at Agnes and her friend shrugged. But Nightshade seemed to have gained control over his emotions enough to look a bit sheepish. "You three can go. But don't leave town. I'm going to have some questions later. Especially about why you thought you had to save Miss Tyne's life."

Even as he said the words, Flo could see the realization entering Nightshade's tiny little mind that there might be something behind their presence there. Since the woman they'd been attempting to warn was currently lying dead in her bedroom.

Flo grabbed Agnes' arm. "Let's go, fool. Hurry up."

"Mrs. Bee?" Nightshade's voice sounded more curious than commanding so she chose to ignore it.

Flo stepped up the pace, urging Jamie forward gently but firmly and pulling Agnes. "Hurry up!" she whispered. By the time they reached the front door, they were nearly running. Fortunately, Nightshade didn't come after them. He was probably thinking, rightfully, that a few moments to gather himself were in order.

They hurried back down the sidewalk toward Flo's car, which was, unfortunately, pinned in by several cop cars, the CSU van, and an ambulance with its lights still flashing. She stood beside her car, looking around, a sinking feeling in her belly. "We're completely blocked in."

Agnes pointed to the narrow strip of flower bed bordering the lawn. "We can just bop right over that and drive across the yard."

Flo frowned. "We'll flatten all the flowers."

Agnes shook her head. "Flo, Melody Tyne is beyond caring if we flatten a few petunias."

Flo looked at Jamie, who was gnawing nervously on a fingernail. The young girl shrugged. "It's not as bad as having somebody puke on your face."

"Or turn your dresser into kindling," Agnes said, chuckling.

"It's not funny," Jamie murmured.

Flo skimmed a look toward the house, hearing Nightshade's voice inside. What if he was coming out?

"Boy, they sure got here fast," Agnes said.

"Who?" Jamie asked.

Agnes pointed toward the street, where a big, old-fashioned hearse was idling. "The mortuary folks. Don't they usually wait until the morgue's done with the body?"

Flo's eyes went wide. "Satan's boogers!" She grabbed the door handle. "Get in the car ladies and make it fast."

Agnes frowned. "Why?"

"Agnes Willard for once will you just do as your told without arguing?"

Agnes' round face folded into a belligerent frown. "I'm not arguing. I'm just asking a reasonable question."

Flo climbed behind the wheel and started the car. "Well then you can stand there and answer yourself too. I'm leaving."

Agnes grabbed the handle and wrenched the door open, barely flinging herself into the back seat before Flo wrenched the wheel to the left and hit the gas. The tires gave a little squeal before they caught hold of the asphalt and surged around, smashing a patch of flowers and two small bushes before the tires found grass. Then she stomped on the gas and shot straight across the grass, headed for the street.

Agnes and Jamie grabbed hold of anything they could find. Jamie's eyes bulged in her pretty face. "What's going on, Mrs. Bee?"

The "hearse" suddenly gunned it and swung out into the street.

Flo barely slowed as she reached the edge of the yard, turning the wheel to follow the big black monstrosity as it bounced and wavered down the street at full speed.

Her wheels bounced over the curb and she went airborne for a beat before they hit the street with a thump and Flo fought the wheel to get them straightened out. Behind them, a car hit the horn, clearly not happy with her emergency dismount from Melody Tyne's yard. She wrapped her hands tightly around the steering wheel and pressed on the gas. "Hold on!"

Ahead of them, the hearse took a turn on two wheels, its tick-like body wobbling dangerously at the end, and then straightened and lumbered off at an unworkable speed.

"He's gonna crash that thing," Jamie said, one hand clutching the dash so hard Flo figured they'd be able to take a picture to get her fingerprints when Nightshade threw them all in jail.

Agnes' big head popped up between them. "I hope he doesn't have a body in the back."

"Seat belts!" Flo screamed as the hearse squealed around another corner a block ahead of them.

Agnes expelled air and disappeared, hopefully to do what she was told and clamp her seatbelt on.

The hearse slowed slightly, still a couple of blocks ahead of them. It appeared to be slowing because the driver could barely maneuver its bulk between the cars parked on both sides of the residential street. Flo relaxed a little, thinking she could catch it. What she was going to do once she caught it was a problem for another time.

But the hearse suddenly turned into a park, hitting the gas and speeding past the large fountain in the center. It disappeared into one of the densely treed park roads. By the time Flo caught up it was nowhere to be found. She wandered around the park for a while, turning down side roads that mostly led to more trees and a few picnic areas, before she admitted she'd lost him.

"He's gone," Flo said.

"Who's gone, Mrs. Bee?" Jamie asked.

Flo sighed. "I'm guessing it was Vlad. Though the windows in that monstrosity are tinted so dark it's impossible to see inside."

Flo heard a smacking sound from the back and turned to see Agnes with a red mark on her forehead. Her friend was shaking her head. "Of course! I should have recognized that hearse."

Jamie grimaced. "You know somebody at the mortuary?"

"That wasn't a mortuary hearse, hun. It was a private one."

Their young friend wrinkled her nose. "Eww."

Agnes shrugged. "It's really more practical than it seems. Vlad and Morty need someplace to store their victims after they drain them dry. They've probably got them stacked up like cordwood back there."

The young reporter sucked air, her pretty brown eyes wide.

"Stop it, Agnes. You're scaring the child."

"I'm not scared, Mrs. Bee."

Flo didn't comment.

"We need to find him, Flo," Agnes said. "If we had any doubt there was a connection between Vlad and Melody Tyne, that's gone bye-bye."

"I agree."

Jamie shook her head. "I'm so confused."

Flo gave her a smile as she turned back out onto Main street and headed for Silver Hills. "Vladwick Newsome is the night manager at Silver Hills. We think he might be the connection we're looking for between *Nightowl, Inc.* and the Tynes."

"Because Melody Tyne was offered a job at Silver Hills?" Jamie shook her head. "That seems thin."

"More importantly, because Vlad and Morty are slum lords. We've known that about them for years. If there's a scandal having to do with slumlordery in Silver City, they're the first ones I'd suspect to be in the center of it."

"And because Vlad just showed up at Melody Tyne's home," Agnes added.

Flo turned into the residence. "But the really interesting thing is that nobody seems to know anything about the woman. Vlad denies having hired her and so does Richard."

"And Vlad ran away when he saw her."

Flo nodded. "Something isn't adding up."

"Maybe Morty hired Melody Tyne."

Flo parked the car and turned off the key. She looked into the rear-view mirror and found Agnes blinking. "We probably should have thought of that," Flo said on a frown. She patted Jamie on the arm. "Nice work, hun."

Jamie grinned. "I've had some experience with investigative reporting. It comes in handy occasionally."

Flo opened her door. "The Newsomes should be here by now. At least one of them..." She frowned, remembering the fleeing hearse in the park. "We'll see if we can find Morty and interrogate her. Maybe by the time we're done Vlad will have shown up."

"Sounds like a plan," Jamie said on a grin. Flo realized the young reporter was enjoying herself.

Well, except for the whole puking on the corpse thing.

And why wouldn't she? If they figured out who killed the two Tyne women, Jamie was going to have herself a whopper of a story to tell.

CHAPTER EIGHT

A MAN WAS COMING OUT of the office as Flo and Agnes approached the door. She frowned when she saw him, something about him vaguely familiar. He fixed a wide, mean-looking gaze on them as he walked past, his manner openly hostile.

She frowned, holding his gaze until he was past her and exiting through the front door.

"Who was that?" Agnes asked with a frown.

"I don't know but I hope he isn't going to be a new tenant at Silver Hills. I really don't like the cut of his jib."

Flo opened the office door and stormed inside, expecting to see Morticia's long, lean, vampiric figure sitting behind her desk, doing whatever creatures of the night did when they took jobs as night managers.

She didn't expect the long, lean vampiric figure who was actually sitting behind the desk. She blinked in surprise. "Vlad."

He glanced up from the hiring folder, his black eyes wary. "Woman from the second floor and her mutant sidekick."

Flo let a small sigh escape. "We need to speak to Morty."

He made a notation on one of the applications and closed the file. "She's not here yet."

"But that's not possible."

Vlad stood up and clasped the folder, fixing his usual look of disgust on her and Agnes. "I was unaware my wife needed to clear her activities with you nitwits."

Flo bristled at the insult but chose to ignore it. After all, they did always accuse him of draining people dry. "How is it that you're here and she's not?"

Vlad made a point of looking to one side and then the other, mimicking surprise. "What a relief. From your stupid question I was momentarily afraid that Morty had become fused to my side." He narrowed his black gaze. "Have you been drinking?"

"Not us," said Agnes. "But maybe you've drained one too many inebriated people today. We just saw you in the park."

"It wasn't me," he said without hesitation. "I came in early to try to put this annoying hiring fiasco to rest."

There was so much in that statement that Flo didn't know where to go first. She decided to go with the most important part. "You picked the two finalists?"

He walked out from behind Morty's desk. "That would be a great big dose of nunya business." He reached for the handle of the inner office door.

"Wait!"

To Flo's surprise, he did stop and slide a bored gaze her way. "Now what?"

"I want to know what your relationship was to Melody Tyne."

She could tell by the determined stillness of his expression that she'd caught him by surprise. He'd clearly been expecting more questions about the job.

"What are you talking about?"

"Melody Tyne," she said again. "The woman you were going to shove down our throats for the weekend manager's position. I want to know how you know her and why you were just at her house."

He sighed as if she was just too exhausting to endure. "I already told you I came in here early. I wasn't at anybody's house just now and I have no idea who this woman...Tyne did you say...is."

"Was," Agnes told him. "She was murdered."

Vlad's bored facade cracked and he looked for a moment as if he was going to fess up. But then the office door opened and a snotty voice said, "You're talking to the wrong Newsome. It was me you saw at Melody Tyne's home."

Flo turned away from Vlad's smug grin to find Morty gliding into the room. As usual, she wore a long, black column dress and black pumps. With her straight black hair and dark eyes, she looked every bit the horror movie monster they'd pegged her. Morty pursed lips covered in blood-red lipstick and shoved the single ribbon of white hair away from her face. "Why are you in here pestering Vlad?"

"Why were you at Melody Tyne's house?"

Morty frowned. "Why is that your business?"

Flo could see why, aside from the obvious reasons, Vlad and Morty got along. "Because it was the scene of a murder and I'm guessing you didn't have a good reason to be there."

Morty's slim black brows rose. "And you did?"

Okay, she had a teensy-weensy point. "We were there on police business."

Morty gave her a look. "Seriously? That's what you're going with?"

Flo shrugged. "You are aware that I work at the Silver City Police Department now."

"As a file clerk, yeah. That hardly qualifies you to interfere at crime scenes."

Flo bristled and then realized what Morty was doing. She forced herself to smile. "You aren't going to get my goat, Morty."

"Yeah," Agnes agreed. "You'll have to use something else as your ritual sacrifice tonight. Flo's not letting you have her goat." She chuckled heartily, clearly happy with herself.

Flo rolled her eyes. "Melody Tyne showed up here yesterday and announced she was one of the finalists for the open manager position. And now she's dead and you were seen at her house."

"I believe you were seen at her house too, Bee. Does that mean you killed her?"

"No, *Newsome*, it doesn't. But I'm not being sued by the dead woman."

If Morty's chalk-white face had been made of porcelain as it appeared, Flo figured she'd have put a few hairline cracks in it. The other woman's lips tightened and three small lines showed up between her midnight colored eyebrows. "Melody Tyne was not suing us."

"Morticia, be quiet!"

Her shark-like gaze snapped to her husband. "I'm sick of being accused of everything that happens around here. Just because we own a few rentals..."

Flo gave a very unladylike snort. "I was inside one of those 'rentals' Morty. It wasn't fit for humans to inhabit." Flo would never forget the apartment she and Agnes had searched when young Yegor Sabitov had shown up dead in the Silver Hills library. They'd gone to his place looking for clues to his murder and had been appalled by the squalor in which he'd lived.

The other woman shrugged. "We can't be held responsible if the renter doesn't take care of the property."

"There was a raccoon in the bathroom!" Agnes shrieked.

Morty slid her cold gaze toward Agnes. "He wasn't supposed to have a pet. He didn't pay the pet deposit."

Flo barely kept from sighing. "Melody Tyne and her mother were suing the company that owned the mother's rental building and now they're both dead. Does that sound like a coincidence to you?"

"And how, exactly does that involve us?" Vlad asked.

Flo whipped around. She'd nearly forgotten he was there. "I already told you that."

He shook his head, lifting his hands as if perplexed. "You've told us nothing that makes any sense."

She fought for calm, knowing that if she went off both Newsomes would be pleased. They lived to make Flo crazy.

"Mr. Newsome, do you own a company named *Nightowl, Inc.*?"

Everyone turned to Jamie, who'd been standing quietly by the door, unnoticed. Vlad glared and Morty fixed her icy gaze on the young reporter. To her credit, Jamie didn't flinch. She stared back at them, waiting.

"We do not own a company by that name," Vlad finally responded.

Flo was shocked he'd even bothered to answer. He had to be aware of Jamie's job and was attempting damage control. She only hoped the young reporter saw through the carefully worded response.

"Do you know who *does* own the company?"

"How would I know that?"

Jamie held his gaze, like a pretty little bulldog. "Because I'm guessing the rental business is a small world in Silver City. It seems likely you'd have bumped up against the owner a time or two."

He frowned but was saved from answering by his wife. "Vlad and I don't own a rental company by that name, and we don't involve ourselves in the business of others." She glided past them and lowered herself into her chair. "I'd recommend you three try to do the same."

Flo knew a dismissal when she heard one. Fortunately, she wasn't good at taking orders. "That doesn't explain how a woman who nobody seems to know showed up declaring she was a finalist for the manager position."

Morty looked shocked. "Is that what this is all about?" She shook her head. "I contacted Miss Tyne and told her she was a finalist. I asked her to come after five so I could speak to her. She must have misinterpreted that to mean after five AM." Morty refolded her porcelain facade into a frown. "You say she's dead? That's unfortunate. I guess I'll have to pick another candidate."

"Don't worry," Agnes told them with a grin. "My application will be in there tonight."

Morty curled her lip. "I'll be sure to look for it so I can assign it to the circular file." She looked at Flo. "You ladies know all about filing, don't you?"

Flo's mouth opened and closed a few times and her hands formed into fists before she decided discretion was the better part of valor and turned on her heel. She should have known she'd never get a straight answer from the Newsomes. She'd have to try a different tack.

Agnes and Jamie caught up with her halfway across the entryway. She was so angry there was a roaring sound in her ears and she didn't hear Jamie calling to her until the young woman ran up and tapped her on the arm. "Mrs. Bee? Are you all right?"

Flo stopped, took a deep breath, and nodded, forcing herself to smile. "I'll be fine, hun. I don't know why I let those two get to me."

Agnes rolled up on Flo's other side. "Because they're demons and they have demonic powers of mind control." She shook her head. "I guess there's no point in submitting my application. Morty will just throw it away."

Anger rose again on the thought. "Oh, you're going to submit it. We'll give it straight to Richard and tell him she's threatened to destroy it. He'll make sure you get fair consideration."

Agnes nodded. "Good idea."

Flo spotted someone in the dining room she needed to speak with and started off again. "Come on, ladies."

"What are we doing?" Jamie asked.

"Engaging Plan B," Flo told her. "If we can't get the information we need from the horse's mouth we'll ask the sheep instead."

"Oh," Agnes said with a grin. "I see the problem. You thought you were talking to the horse's mouth. Alas, you were addressing the other end."

Jamie snorted.

Flo just shook her head and curved her lips into something that hopefully resembled a sincere smile. "Hello, gentlemen."

Bill, Bob and Bo Baccarat looked up, their eyes going wide as the three women approached their table. The men shoved awkwardly at the checkers set in front of them on the table and pushed to their feet, their assorted beady brown gazes sliding toward the general vicinity of Flo and Co without actually landing on them. In their mid-forties and socially awkward to an extreme, the three men were fraternal triplets with unfortunate looks to go with their unfortunate names. They looked a lot like the three stooges and, despite the fact that they were unfunny to the extreme, the triplets often found themselves mired in the slapstick comedy of their doppelgangers just through sheer awkwardness.

At least they had an excuse, thought Flo. Agnes was mired in slapstick and she was socially normal.

Mostly.

The leader of the three brothers was Bill. His cap of dark brown hair wasn't quite as long as the infamous Moe's but it was shaped just as weirdly, like an upside-down bowl on his head. His bushy brown eyebrows danced as he inclined his head, making him look like he was leering at her even as he flushed with embarrassment. "Mrs. Bee."

She reached out and took his fleshy hand in hers, giving it a squeeze. "How are you Bill?"

He skimmed a quick look at his brothers as if to ask them how he was. Flo didn't know how the whole triplet thing worked, but she figured he should have known how he was without their help.

She smiled at Bob and Bo. "It looks like you three are having a riveting round of checkers."

Their features folded into something that looked like confusion and Flo nearly sighed with frustration. How was it possible that Vlad the Repeller had managed to have a conversation with the three brothers and she couldn't even wring out of them how they were feeling? Flo didn't understand how the three brothers managed to move through their lives. Suddenly she wondered what they did for a living. She thought she remembered hearing that one of them did some kind of business training or mentoring on the side. She couldn't imagine it. But maybe they were more comfortable dealing with subjects they knew a lot about.

Jamie stepped forward, pulling a small notepad from the pocket of her sweater. "Hello. My name is Jamie Poyrie. I work for the Silver City Tribune."

Flo's hand fluttered at her side as she instinctively thought about stopping her young friend. If a friendly overture terrified the men, Jamie's *take no prisoners* manner would surely send them into convulsions. To Flo's eternal shock, all three men grew serious and intent, focused carefully on her words as she explained how she was doing an expose on a local company named *Nightowl, Inc.* and she wondered if she could ask them some questions.

Bob nodded his frizzy gray head. "Of course, young woman. But I've never heard of them."

Flo felt her eyes go wide. The entire time she'd known the brothers, she'd never heard Bob string more than two words together at a time. "It's a rental company," she told them. They swung matching brown gazes in her direction and frowned. Bo lifted his hand. "We don't believe in renting," he told Flo as if he was discussing the effects of fossil fuels on the earth.

"He's right," Bill agreed quickly. "Renting is a waste of money."

Flo was at a loss. "But don't you rent your apartment here?"

The brothers shared a look, clearly as perplexed by their own statements as Flo was. Finally, Bo shook his head. "This is home."

And there it was. Despite the incongruity of their stances, Flo completely understood.

"Did you gentlemen know a Melissa or Melody Tyne?" Jamie asked them.

All three men shook their heads.

Jamie looked at Flo.

"We saw you speaking to Vladwick Newsome on the street. Can you tell us what that was about?"

Bob lowered bushy gray brows and cocked his head. "Nope."

She blinked, surprised beyond words.

Jamie lifted her notebook, poising her pencil over the empty page. "It's important."

"Why?" Bo asked.

"Um..." Jamie scanned Flo a silent plea for help.

"We think Vlad's working with a slumlord company that's killing people," Agnes blurted out unhelpfully.

All three men paled with shock. Bo was the first to recover. "That's crazy talk."

Flo glared over at Agnes and her friend glared back. "There's no point dancing around the issue, Flo. If Vlad's responsible for the deaths of those poor women we need to know it sooner rather than later."

Bo gasped.

Bob bristled.

Bill gulped. "Murder? You can't be serious."

Flo shook her head, going into damage control. "That's not what Agnes is implying..."

"Vlad murdered somebody?"

Flo barely kept from groaning aloud as Elisa Kemp, Silver Hills' non-official rumor queen hurried over. She'd apparently had her big ears scanning the room for gossip and had overheard Agnes' charge. She stopped in front of Flo, looking down her beak-like nose and licking her lips as if anticipating a tasty tidbit.

"Well, it could be Morty I guess," Agnes added.

Eliza slammed a hand over her heart, gasping theatrically. "You think Morty killed someone?"

"Oh, good heavens," Flo muttered. The absolute worst thing that could happen was for Eliza Kemp to start spreading rumors that the Newsome twosome were murderers. That would get their nascent investigation shut down faster than TC could type Rumpelstiltskin into the pages of one of her murder mysteries. "Agnes didn't mean that. She was just wondering why Vlad was going around chatting it up with people..."

Eliza lowered judgmental eyebrows at Flo. "You're accusing them of murder just because he was talking to somebody?"

"Eliza, this is Vlad," Flo said.

The gossip queen gave that a moment's thought and then nodded. "Ah, I see your point."

Bill blew out a frustrated sigh. "He was just being friendly..." The man stopped mid-sentence and blinked. Then he frowned. "Oh. Yeah. I see the problem."

"He didn't ask you for anything?" Flo asked.

"Not really, no."

"What does 'not really' mean?" Agnes asked.

"He just wanted to make sure we were going to come to the panel the night we vote for manager. He said it was important for everyone to be there."

Flo frowned. That didn't make any sense at all. Unless he was planning on pushing a certain candidate. But if that was his aim, he should have mentioned someone. "Did he give you a name of a candidate to consider?"

Bill shook his head. "Nope."

"I wasn't aware they'd selected any candidates yet," Eliza said.

"They picked one but now she's dead," Agnes blurted.

Flo sighed.

Eliza looked at her. "Is that true, Flo?"

"Of course it's true," Agnes said, bristling. "I wouldn't lie about that."

"Yes. It is true," Flo verified. "Her mother's dead too. We believe their deaths are tied to a lawsuit against a slumlord rental organization."

"Oh my." Eliza smoothed a long-fingered hand over the slicked back hair on top of her head. As usual, the dark strands were corralled in a death grip at the back of her long neck and twisted into an efficient bun. "This is terrifying. How many people were included in that suit?"

Flo stilled, her pulse picking up as she realized they hadn't even checked. What if there were others listed in the suit? They'd be in danger too. "I don't know."

Eliza widened her small eyes and clasped her throat theatrically. "You need to find out!"

Yes. They did. And Flo knew just the man who could help them.

CHAPTER NINE

"WHAT IN THE WORLD HAVE you gotten yourself mixed up in now, doll?"

"To be fair, Roger, this all just kind of fell into our laps."

He eyed her with a skeptical blue gaze. "You don't honestly expect me to believe that, do you? I *have* met you and Agnes."

She tightened her lips against a grin. "Point taken. But I am being mostly honest. We did go to the scene of the first murder but it was only because we thought it was Melody Tyne..."

"Tell me again who that is?"

"Apparently she's the woman Morty selected to take the weekend manager's position."

His eyes widened. "You don't say. Well, I can see why you'd be interested in her murder." He thought about it for a moment and then his handsome face smoothed into a neutral mask. He cleared his throat and looked at Agnes. "You aren't by any chance killing off the competition are you, Agnes?"

Agnes twitched in surprise and then bristled, her jaw tightening until she saw him fighting a grin. Then she smiled. "You're very bad, Roger Attles."

He gave a little chuckle. "I know I shouldn't have but I couldn't resist." He winked at Flo and she shook her head.

"Poor Jamie will never be the same after finding that body."

The amused glint left Roger's gaze. "You're right, doll. I'm sorry."

She shook her head.

"Don't feel too badly, Roger," Agnes offered. "I think she's mostly suffering from guilt for having horked all over the body."

"No!"

Agnes nodded. "Yep."

He looked down, scrubbing a hand over his jaw. When he looked up again the amused glint had left his eyes and the blue was steely again. "Tell me what you need from me."

"We think the Tynes were killed because they were leading a class action suit against a company named *Nightowl, Inc.*"

"You want me to find out what I can about this company?"

"That would be wonderful," she told him. "If you can find anything out you'll be doing better than young Jamie. She's been trying to dig into them for the expose she's writing."

Roger's head came up and he looked around the lobby. "Where is young Jamie? I saw her with you earlier."

"She took an Uber back to her office. She has work to do on this story."

"It looks like Miss Jamie's story will be more than an expose," he pointed out. "Now that murder appears to be part of it."

"That's true." Flo frowned. "I hope they don't take the story away from her."

"She *is* young. This narrative might benefit from a more experienced hand."

"That's why we're helping her," Agnes told him proudly.

"Yes." He cleared his throat, winking at Flo again.

She tried to look exasperated with him but she just couldn't dredge anything up. He was always a delight to be around despite the circumstances. It was one of the things she loved about him. "We'll do our best to make sure she stays on the story. We're hoping you can help us with that."

He nodded. "I'll visit the firm today and see what I can find out. Arthur might know something about this class action suit that will be helpful." Arthur Janick had been Roger's partner in their law firm, Janick, Attles and Benedick. Devon Benedick had since passed away, leaving the firm to his two partners. When Roger retired he sold his half of the company to Arthur, but he still kept an office there in case he needed it. His expertise and the law office's large cache of past and present legal documents had come in very handy during Flo's investigative efforts.

"There's one other thing, hun."

Roger fixed a serious gaze on her. "What's that?"

"If this company is systematically murdering the plaintiffs in the class action suit, anyone else who's listed on it might be in danger."

"Ah. You're right, doll. I guess I'd better get a move on then." He reached out and grabbed her hand, giving it a squeeze. "Shall we debrief over steaks at *Beefeater's* tonight?"

"Yes!" Agnes declared excitedly. "I've been starving for a steak."

Flo didn't have the heart to tell Agnes she didn't think that was exactly what Roger had in mind. Bless his kind heart, he didn't burst her friend's bubble.

"It's a date then." He winked at Flo again and left, his long strides quickly eating up the space to the front entrance.

"He didn't mean me, did he?" Agnes asked sheepishly.

"Of course he did, hun. Roger loves spending time with you."

She snorted. "You're a terrible liar. But I'm still coming to the restaurant with you. I wasn't lying about craving a steak."

Flo grinned. "I have to admit it's been too long since we were there..." Flo's phone rang and she looked at it. "It's Jamie." Pressing the button to accept the call, Flo said, "Jamie. Are you okay?"

"I'm fine. But I have some really bad news. Can you guys meet me at the diner?"

"Of course, hun. We'll be there in twenty minutes."

JAMIE WAS SITTING AT a back booth when they entered *Frankie's Place*. Her pops, the infamous Frankie, waved to them from behind the counter, where he was taking the orders of a family of four while managing the busy window into the kitchen. Flo caught him glancing toward his daughter as they moved on past, no doubt wishing she'd decided to go into the family business rather than becoming a reporter.

The young journalist looked up as they approached, her gaze sliding around the diner as if looking for danger.

Flo frowned, wondering what had the young woman so spooked. "Hey, hun."

Jamie gave them a tight smile. "Ladies. Did you find out what we need from Roger?"

"Not yet, hun. He's at the firm right now trying to find it."

She nodded. "Good. That's good." She scanned the diner again, her fingers twitching nervously toward her coffee mug and then going still as she realized the mug was empty. She squirmed in her seat, glancing nervously toward her father, who was fetching a bunch of plates filled with steaming food from the pass thru window.

Flo and Agnes sat down across from Jamie. A beat later, Frankie appeared with the coffee pot. "Hey, ladies."

"Frankie, how are you?" Flo asked.

"Keepin' busy." He reached out and gave his daughter's shoulder a squeeze. "Sure could use some help."

"I told you, I'm busy, pops!" Jamie snapped.

Her pops took the snappish response in his stride, merely giving her shoulder another squeeze before turning to Flo. "I hope you ladies can help her figure out whatever's ridin' her tail. She's not fit ta be around right now."

Jamie sighed. "Sorry, pops. It's just this story I'm working. The editor's trying to take it away from me."

Frankie lifted twin black brows. "You ain't gonna let that happen are ya, baby girl." It wasn't really a question. It seemed more like a firm suggestion.

"No, I'm not, pops."

He nodded. "You ladies want pie?"

"That would be wonderful, hun."

He glanced at Agnes. She was chewing her lip.

It wasn't like her to hesitate about pie. Agnes was the original baked goods fanatic. She never turned down anything sweet or baked. Frankie figured out what the problem was immediately. He grinned. "Ain't no rhubarb today, cher. We got sugar cream and cherry." Agnes had been roped into eating rhubarb pie at *Frankie's* once and she hated it. She clearly wasn't going to make that mistake again.

Agnes grinned. "Sugar cream please."

Flo nodded. "That sounds perfect."

He looked at his daughter. She turned an impatient gaze his way. "Nothing for me, pops. Thanks."

Jamie watched her father walk away before grabbing her oversized, black leather purse and shoving her hand inside. She handed Flo a printed story and sat back, watching carefully as Flo scanned it. Halfway down the page, Flo saw a name that made her stomach twist with nerves. "Satan's boogers!"

Jamie all but bounced in her seat. "Right?"

"What is it? What do you see?" Agnes asked. She scanned the article and frowned. "Who's Parks Buddrick?"

Flo gave her a look. "Flip that around and change it a bit."

Agnes seemed to be straining to figure it out for a moment and then her eyes went wide. "Yikes!"

"What is it you ladies are working on?" Frankie asked as he placed their slices of pie in front of them.

Flo skimmed Jamie a look and the young woman gave a quick jerk of her head. Flo wasn't surprised. If Frankie knew the cultist was back he'd have a conniption fit.

Fortunately blabber mouth Agnes was too busy diving into her pie to spill the beans.

"Nothing all that interesting," Jamie told her pops. "Just a slumlord case."

Frankie nodded. But the look he gave Flo made her palms sweat. He was looking her right in the eye, all but daring her to lie to him. Clearly, he didn't believe his daughter.

Flo had no choice but to dive into her pie too. With a full mouth she couldn't be made to lie. She chewed the all too big bite and stared back at Frankie, watching suspicion slide through his brown gaze. Finally, he shook his head. "All right then. You girls be good now, y'hear?"

Agnes saluted and Frankie left, chuckling.

Jamie leaned across the table. "We shouldn't have met here." She chewed her lip and glanced around the homey little restaurant. "It's just..."

"You feel safe here," Flo said, completely understanding.

Jamie nodded, rubbing her arms. "He can't find out about this," she told them.

"He won't find out from us," Flo said. "Right, Agnes?"

Agnes was scraping the last of her pie off her plate and starting to eye Flo's. "Mmm fmmbf."

"You really should tell him, though, hun. He'll support you. But if you didn't tell him and you got hurt..."

She sighed. "I know. I probably will. Just not right now. I need time to let it sink in first."

"I know what you mean," Flo told her. "I thought he'd left town."

"This is his MO. He goes underground until things die down and then he remakes himself and comes back."

"Another cult?" Agnes asked.

"Not that I know of," Jamie said. "Just this scammy business the article talks about."

Flo shook her head. "Home security? That's a bit like hiring a shark as a lifeguard."

Agnes reached for Flo's plate. "You gonna eat this?"

Flo shoved the plate toward her friend. "I'm saving room for steak tonight."

"Me too," Agnes agreed. "That's why I didn't get ice cream."

Jamie shook her head, watching Agnes tuck into the second slice of pie with awe on her face. "I don't know how you can eat when the world is about to end."

"Now, hun. It's not that bad. We'll just tell Detectives Nightshade and Peters that Buddy Parks is back in town. They'll keep an eye on him."

"I don't think you understand, Mrs. Bee. If Parks is here there's a pretty good chance he's tied up in this *Nightowl, Inc.* mess."

"Did you find a connection?"

"Not yet," Jamie said, looking gloomy. "But I know he's involved somehow."

Flo shook her head. "I don't know..."

"I feel it in my gut, Mrs. Bee. And my instincts are rarely wrong."

Flo thought about Parks, the evil genius behind a series of cults that had lured unsuspecting people, mostly young men and women, into his clutches and then twisted their minds while getting them to do terrible things that would change their lives forever. She couldn't escape the memory of the deaths which could be tied directly to those cults. Flo and Agnes had barely escaped with their lives the last time they'd gone up against him.

And Jamie had almost lost everything.

"We'll get to the bottom of this, hun. I promise."

"I hope you're right," Jamie told her, looking miserable. "Because, whether he's involved in this *Nightowl* mess or not, we're all in danger until he's behind bars."

"WHERE TO NOW?" AGNES asked as they headed back toward town.

"We're going to talk to Nightshade." Agnes groaned and Flo shot her a look. "And you're going to behave yourself."

"Then maybe I should stay in the car because that man steps on my last nerve and engages my punching reflex."

Flo shook her head. "You let him get to you. Don't do it."

"That's easy for you to say. You haven't experienced the unique and invigorating pleasure of punching him."

Flo fought a grin. "There is that."

Detective Brent Peters was heading into the bullpen when they came through the front door of the Silver City Police Department. He screeched to a halt and stood there, frowning. "You're not scheduled to work in the dungeon today."

"You see, I knew there was a reason you were a detective." Agnes said with a smug grin. "We just can't slide anything past you."

"Agnes, behave," Flo murmured. "We need to speak to Detective Nightshade."

"About what?"

"About a case he's working," Flo said evasively. "We have information for him."

Peters arched a dark gold brow. "Really? Well, that's refreshing. Usually you're withholding information so you can pursue an investigation behind our backs."

"Hearsay and lies," Agnes sniffed.

"Okay, Perry Mason." He shook his head. "Nightshade's not here. He went home with the flu. Guess who inherited his caseload?"

Flo barely held back a groan. "Oh. That's...wonderful."

He chuckled. "And that was very insincere." He jerked his head toward the door. "Come on. You can fill me in."

He motioned them to a couple of hard wooden chairs on the other side of his desk and eased into his chair. He leaned back to the screeching whine of the ancient desk chair and crossed his arms over his chest. "Talk to me."

Flo barely restrained a sigh. She'd hoped to share a little information to get a little information but she knew Detective Peters too well to expect that he'd play that game. She'd have to be cagey. "It's come to our attention that the cultist, Buddy Parks, is back in Silver City."

Peters didn't look surprised. "Buddy Parks, huh? And you know this how?"

Flo didn't want to bring Jamie into it for several reasons, most of all because the young girl was a direct target of Parks'. "I can't reveal my source..."

He laughed. "You're not Woodward or Bernstein Mrs. Bee. Tell me how you know."

Flo decided a half-truth would suffice. "I read it in the business section of today's paper. A man named Parks Buddrick is opening a new security business in Silver City. Apparently, he's targeting renters with a new, transferrable security system."

Peters stared at her for a long moment and then leaned forward, placing his hands on top of his desk as if preparing to rise. "Thanks for coming in today, Mrs. Bee. It was nice seeing you."

"You're going to ignore my information?"

"What information? It's obvious that you're just reciting knowledge that's publicly available." He shrugged, dismissing it and her.

"Buddy Parks is a dangerous man."

"Parks may or may not be dangerous. We can't pin anything on him except trying to run a self-help organization in Silver City. As far as we know he did nothing wrong. His daughter took all the responsibility for everything else."

"You don't really believe that, do you?"

Peters shrugged. It was clear to Flo that he was not going to share what he did or did not believe. "And furthermore, you don't even know if this Buddrick guy is the same guy..."

"Oh, come on, Detective Peters," Agnes said, curling her lip in disgust. "I thought you were smarter than that."

He glared over at her for a beat before going on. "And even if it is, we need what he's offering. Those people he's targeting with his security product are desperate. There's been a wave of break-ins at those buildings. Until the *Rest Easy* product came on the market, renters haven't had much recourse unless they wanted to spend hundreds of dollars to wire up a security system that they'll lose and continue to pay for if they moved. That's not exactly a workable option for these folks. They don't have the kind of money needed to sign up for one of the big security companies. Buddrick is offering them real security at a time when they desperately need it."

"You're not even concerned that he's using a false name?" Flo couldn't believe what she was hearing. No wonder the Silver City police had never been able to bring Buddy Parks down. They were apparently susceptible to his lies and charm.

"Again, are you sure he's using a fake name?"

Flo's mouth opened and hung there. She was too shocked to respond. Could the police really be so stupid?

Detective Peters stood up and gave her a conciliatory look. "I know you suffered at the hands of this cult." He scanned a look toward Agnes to include her. "Both of you did. But I can assure you we've done all we can, legally to make sure Parks Buddrick..."

"Buddy Parks," Flo said through gritted teeth.

"—or whatever he's calling himself, is on the up and up. As much as you might not like it, he's providing a legitimate service that Silver City needs right now. We don't have the manpower to protect all the renters in the city. I wish we did."

Flo stood up and gave him a mulish look. "Fine. If you won't try to stop this evil man, we will." She turned on her heel and strode toward the door, ignoring him as he called out to her.

Agnes stomped along beside her, flinging the front door open and storming outside. "I can't believe how stubborn that man is."

Flo was too angry to speak. She just shook her head and headed for her car, her mind spinning.

When they were in the car, Agnes turned to Flo. "The best chance we have of taking Parks down is to prove he's part of *Nightowl, Inc.*"

Flo stared straight ahead, her teeth grinding together and her knuckles white on the steering wheel. She thought about Agnes' suggestion for a moment and then came to a decision. She felt better almost immediately. Turning to Agnes, she nodded. "You're right. We need to tie him to *Nightowl, Inc.*"

"How are we gonna do that?" Agnes asked almost to herself.

"There's only one way. We're going to stake the place out and get photo evidence."

CHAPTER TEN

"REALLY, AGNES? YOU know we're only going to be there a couple of hours, right?"

Agnes shoved the third bag of groceries into the back seat and climbed in next to it. Flo figured it was the first time in her life Agnes hadn't fought for shotgun in the car. "Flo, you know I have a blood sugar problem. This is just a few things to make sure my head is clear in case I need to think fast." She pulled a box of Snow Globe snack cakes from the box and opened it, digging in for two of the sugary treats and ripping open the cellophane surrounding them.

"If you eat all that sugar you're going to be in a coma. Then I really will be on my own."

Agnes blew a raspberry and coconut flakes spewed into the front seat, sticking to Flo's bouff. "Stop that, fool!"

The passenger side door opened and TC slipped into the car. Flo was surprised to see her. "Hey, hun. What are you doing?"

TC leveled a quelling look at Flo, skimming it to the back seat and stopping with shock and awe at what was going down back there. "I'm here to make sure you two don't get into trouble." She grimaced. "I've never seen anybody shove that much food into their face at once. It's fascinating in a terrifying way."

"Mffmff, mlfbfb," Agnes said. More crumbs hit the back of Flo's bouff and she sighed. "I can't believe I'm going on a stakeout with the abominable sugar monster."

"Maybe we should get tarps," TC suggested.

"Mff, blmff!" Agnes responded in disgust.

Flo shook her head. "You don't want to get involved in this, hun. Brent's taken over the case."

TC jerked backward, one hand flying up as a chocolate chip flew in her direction, pinging off her palm. "He's the one who sent me to watch over you."

Flo's eyes went wide. "Seriously?"

"Mmff dlfm bliff mmmf?" Agnes exclaimed.

TC scraped crumbs off her face with a grimace. "I refuse to keep talking to you if you don't stop eating."

Flo glanced in the rear-view mirror to find Agnes swallowing the mother lode in her mouth. "I said, I can't believe you're going to spy on us."

TC arched her brows. "And I told you exactly what I was doing. Which makes me a pretty terrible spy, doesn't it?"

Agnes shrugged, lifting a cookie toward her mouth.

"Don't! Do. It." TC said.

Agnes looked at the cookie and sighed, lowering it again. "Okay, but if I faint from low blood sugar it's on you."

Shaking her head, TC turned in her seat and snapped her seat belt on. "Let's go."

"Are you sure, hun?"

"Perfectly sure. Well...almost perfectly. Okay, not even close, but I'm doing this."

Flo started her car and headed out of the lot. She drove down Main street toward town. "Does Brent really know you're here?"

"Would I lie to you?"

No. Flo didn't think TC would. "And he knows what we're doing?"

"Not precisely, no. But he knows you're going to pry into the *Nightowl* thing so he sent me with some guidelines."

"Which are?"

"We watch, document and report back. We don't under any circumstances engage with any of the involved parties, particularly Mr. Buddrick. And no matter what we see, we are not to get out of this car. For any reason."

Flo thought they could mostly work with that.

"I didn't bring any writing material," Agnes lamented from the back as she dug noisily in the bags. She came up with a bag of potato chips. "Maybe we can write on this."

TC frowned. "What are you talking about, Agnes?"

"You said we're supposed to document what we see. I'm envisioning an hourly journal." Agnes was warming to her subject. "It will be fun. We'll be deep cover...keeping a record of our travails as we immerse ourselves in the dangerous territory of our prey. We can even come up with a special code for our reports."

"A moist cookie crumb for A, a greasy piece of potato chip for B...etc.?"

"That would work," Agnes responded with a nod.

TC held up one hand, gaily painted fingernails tapping the surface of her phone. "Or we could just take pictures."

Agnes' wide face folded into a frown and then transformed into a happy smile as she thought about it. "I like that better. Photo evidence can be used in court." She pulled out her flip phone. "I'll do it."

"Does that thing even take pictures," Flo asked. She was pretty sure Agnes' flip phone was almost as old as Agnes was.

"I think it does," Agnes said. She flipped it open and peered at the buttons. "Where would the picture button be?"

TC sighed. "We'll use my phone." Before she realized what Agnes was going to do, her friend had reached over the seat and snatched the phone from TC's hand. "Hey!"

"I'm in charge of the evidence," Agnes told her.

"Nothing can go wrong with that plan," Flo muttered under her breath. She pulled to the curb across the street from the office building where *Nightowl, Inc.* was housed.

TC gave her a grin before instructing Agnes to be careful with her phone. "And don't get food all over it."

Agnes rolled her eyes. "We should peruse the parking lot for the hearse."

Flo stared across the street for a minute, trying to figure out the best way to keep an eye on *Nightowl, Inc.* "Do you suppose this whole building belongs to *Nightowl*?"

TC shook her head. "See that sign there? It lists several businesses."

"Oh. I didn't notice that. Good eye, Miss Colombo."

TC shook her head. "I'm glad I could be of assistance."

Crunching sounds emerged from the back seat. They turned to find Agnes with crumbs all over her face, her cheeks bulging, and her fingers, as she crammed another mouthful of cheesy crisps into her face were neon orange. She stopped chewing as they both made sounds of disgust and lifted her bushy brows. "Bwhath?" Wet orange bits flew toward Flo. She ducked behind the headrest. "Agnes!"

Her friend opened her mouth again to respond but Flo held up a hand. "Swallow first!"

"Give me my phone right now," TC demanded.

Frowning, Agnes reached for the phone and TC squealed, no doubt realizing it would be coated in orange crumbs if Agnes picked it up. "No, don't! Just leave it on the seat."

Agnes frowned and crammed another fistful of the snack into her face.

"Look alive, ladies. It's popo."

TC turned around in her seat, sitting stiffly forward and staring out the windshield as a police car glided slowly past. The woman in the passenger seat wore a uniform and had her red hair pulled back from her face in a tight ponytail. She eyed them suspiciously. Agnes waved, grinning widely. "That's Ginger and Robald," she said excitedly.

Agnes started to lower the window and Flo panicked. "No, fool! We don't want them to ask us why we're here."

"Why not? Detective Peters knows we're here."

"He suspects we might be doing something similar to this but he doesn't know for sure and if these two report back that we're here he just might decide to have them bring us in..."

Regrettably, the cop car slid to a stop and backed up until it was even with Flo's car. She forced a smile onto her face and waved. "Agnes, when I open this window I want you to remind them that they owe you that money."

Crunching sounds floated from the back seat and Flo closed her eyes, wanting to scream. She turned her fake smile on Ginger. "Officer. How are you today?"

The woman slid her green gaze over Flo and Agnes and then skimmed it to TC. "Ladies. You shouldn't loiter here. Somebody in those homes might report you."

Flo turned to look at the buildings alongside the street. Sure enough, though there were office buildings across the road, the buildings on their side were all residences. "Oh. I hadn't noticed."

Ginger frowned. "What are you doing here, anyway?"

Flo turned around in her seat and glared at Agnes. Her friend looked perplexed as she sucked on an orange finger with orange lips. Flo mouthed, *Money* but Agnes merely squinted at her.

"Mrs. Bee?"

Flo turned back to the cop. "We have business in one of those buildings over there."

"What kind of business?"

Flo struggled to come up with something plausible. TC finally saved her.

Sort of.

"I have an appointment with the podiatrist." She grimaced and flung up her foot, nearly kicking Flo in the head. "I think I have Plantar fasciitis."

Ginger made a face. "My sister had that. She said it was really painful."

TC made the appropriate face of misery and nodded. "I'm really in pain."

Robald leaned forward to peer at them from around Ginger. "Then maybe you should park closer to the podiatrist's office." He narrowed his gaze suspiciously. "What are you *really* doing here?"

Flo swung around and said in a harsh whisper, "Money, fool!"

Agnes's eyes widened in final comprehension. She stuck her head out the window. "Money, fools!"

"Oh good Lord," Flo murmured.

Ginger said, "Huh?"

Robald reached for his cuffs. "Did she just call us fools?"

Flo turned around. "Agnes!"

"I mean, did you two come to pay me the money you owe me?"

Ginger went so pale her freckles looked like a reverse star system against her chalky face. She turned to Robald and he flinched. Suddenly Ginger turned back. "We've got to go...emergency..."

Robald flipped on the siren and, faster than Agnes could say, low blood sugar, they were tearing off down the street.

Flo rested her head back on the seat with a relieved sigh.

"That was close," TC murmured.

Flo became aware of a heavy weight in her lap and looked down. TC's long, slender foot was sitting on her thighs. "Um, hun, I think you can move your foot now."

"Oh." TC chuckled. "Sorry. But that was quick thinking, huh?"

"Good lie," Agnes told her. "Except for the fact that the nearest podiatrist's office is at least two miles from here."

TC's smile died. "Well, they didn't know that."

"No," Flo said thoughtfully, "But they had a point. If we're going to see anything interesting in that building we need to get closer." She started her car and put it in gear. "Let's park in the lot. We can see the door better from there."

They pulled across the street and entered the lot. Flo drove up and down the aisles looking for the hearse before she backed her sedan into a spot at the back of the parking lot, facing the building.

Flo realized a potential problem right away. "The office entrances are inside." She gave TC a worried glance. "We're not going to see much from out here."

"No, Flo! Brent said we couldn't approach."

"We won't approach, hun. Just observe."

"And document," Agnes said, lifting TC's crumb-crusted cell phone.

"Ugh!" TC said when she saw her phone. "Give me that back, Agnes."

Agnes yanked the phone away from TC's fingers, slipping it into her pocket. "I told you, TC. I'm in charge of documentation."

They sat in unhappy silence for several minutes, the quiet only broken by the popping of cans as Agnes washed down her snack marathon with liquids. "You two want something to eat or drink?"

TC's stomach rumbled unhappily and she placed a hand over it. "I don't suppose you have a salad in there?"

"Salad isn't stakeout food, TC."

"Who says?"

"I do," Agnes declared.

Shaking her head, TC countered with, "I demand to see the rules of eating on a stakeout."

"I don't have them with me but I'll give them to you after the stakeout."

TC shook her head and silence reigned for a few more minutes.

The car shook as Agnes shifted in her seat. A beat later it shook again. And again. And again.

Flo finally jerked around to glare at her friend. "What is your issue?"

"I really need to pee."

"Oh no!" TC started shaking her head. "Let's take her to the gas station."

But Flo knew an opportunity when she saw one, and she grabbed hold with both hands. "Actually, I need to use the ladies room too and I'm not going to a nasty gas station to do it."

TC groaned. "Flo..."

"You can stay here if you want to, TC. We'll be right back."

Agnes was already out of the car, dancing from foot to foot. "Hurry up!"

Flo reached in and grabbed her purse as TC made a sound of disgust and wrenched the door open. "Okay, let's go. There's no way I'm letting you two out of my sight."

FLO SCANNED THE BRASS wall plaque as they entered the cool, quiet building. *Nightowl, Inc.* was on the first floor and, as they hurried down the marble floored hallway, she saw that it was right next to the ladies room. Fate was clearly sending them a message.

TC noticed where Flo's gaze had landed and started shaking her head. "Not a chance. Brent will kill me. He'll kill us all."

Flo frowned. "I wish Nightshade was still in charge of this case."

"Don't we all," TC sighed. "Go on and do your business. I'll watch the door from here and if I see anything I'll call you."

Flo nodded. "I won't be long." She turned around. "Come on, Agnes..." She was talking to an empty hallway. Agnes had already disappeared. Shaking her head, Flo went into the Ladies room, figuring her friend would already be inside. Sure enough, as Flo selected a stall, Agnes came out, sighing heavily. "Whoo, that was close."

"TMI, hun," Flo told her.

She heard the sound of water running as she did her business and, when she came out, Agnes was eying a large grate high on the wall. "What's wrong? Did you see a spider or something?"

Agnes shook her head. "I was just wondering if that vent goes to the office next door."

Flo washed her hands. "It doesn't matter if it does. You'll never fit in there and I'm certainly not going inside."

Agnes skimmed Agnes a look. "TC could do it."

Flo yanked a paper towel from the machine and chuckled. "There's no way you're going to talk her into that."

"She'd do it if the alternative was us going inside the office."

Flo stilled. Agnes was right. But that meant they'd have to threaten their friend into doing something she would never do otherwise. "TC would never forgive us."

Agnes frowned. She'd been on the wrong side of TC's anger a few times and it wasn't a fun place to be. The last time she'd annoyed TC by disrupting a crime scene when TC had been tasked by her boyfriend, Brent Peters to keep an eye on it, TC had made Agnes take yoga behind Celia Angonetti for a whole week. Agnes's hair still showed signs of the resulting gas-burn. "What if we promised to take whatever we discovered right to the detective. That way we'd be helping him instead of getting in his way."

Flo thought about it for a minute. By sending them TC, Detective Peters had given them kind of unspoken consent to observe and report back. "I guess it wouldn't hurt to ask." Flo threw Agnes a look. "But you have to let me do the talking."

Agnes nodded. "Promise."

The bathroom door opened and TC stuck her head inside. "Buddy Parks just went inside."

Flo's eyes went wide. "He didn't see you, did he?"

She shook her dark head. "I ducked into the snack area across the hall."

"Did you get pictures?" Agnes asked hopefully.

TC glared at her. "With the phone that you wouldn't give back to me?"

"Oh," Agnes said, flushing. "Sorry about that."

Flo motioned TC into the restroom. "Come on in, hun. We have something we need to talk to you about."

CHAPTER ELEVEN

"THERE'S NO WAY YOU'RE going to talk me into that," TC exclaimed, vigorously shaking her head.

"Brent wanted us to observe and document, hun."

She gave Flo a look. "I'm pretty sure he didn't expect us to climb through the ventilation system."

"Why should we be limited by his lack of imagination?" Agnes asked.

Flo sent her a quelling look. "Look, TC, he said you should keep *us* away from *Nightowl*. But he didn't say anything about *you* staying away, did he?"

She frowned. "No."

"And if you can get the information we need, Agnes and I won't be tempted to go inside ourselves."

TC glared down at Flo. "You cannot go into that office. It's not an option."

"I agree. That's why we came up with this idea, hun." Flo could feel her friend softening to the scheme. She bit her tongue to keep from going in for the kill. TC was a wonderful friend, who would do anything for them. But she and Flo shared one personality trait that could sometimes prove difficult. She didn't like to be pushed into doing anything.

TC eyed the grate again. "I don't like this."

"I know, hun." Flo patted her arm. "But we're worried about more people getting killed. And with Parks involved, Jamie might be in the crosshairs."

TC chewed her lip.

"It will be fun," Agnes told her. "And after just a couple of minutes in that vent, you can give your boyfriend definite proof that Parks is involved with *Nightowl.*"

Flo nodded.

Sighing, TC glared at them both. "I'm not happy about this."

"But you'll do it for Jamie?" Flo asked.

"Yes. Ugh! Somebody needs to watch the hallway to make sure he doesn't leave while I'm trying to climb into this thing."

Flo nodded. "I'll do that. Agnes can give you a leg up." She moved to the door and opened it a crack, peering into the empty hallway. "Coast is clear."

"Okay, how are we going to do this?" TC asked, eying the distance to the vent skeptically.

Agnes skimmed a look over the area too. "I figure that thing's about ten feet above our heads. This counter will get us a few feet closer. I'll lift you from there."

TC sighed. "Okay. Let's get it over with." She looked at Flo. "Don't let anybody into this room."

"Not a soul," Flo agreed.

TC made quick work of hopping up onto the counter.

Agnes tried to jump up and hit the side, sliding down and landing in a puffy puddle on the floor. "This might be harder than I thought."

Shaking her head, TC offered Agnes her hand. "Come on, I'll give you a pull."

Flo didn't like the sound of that. Agnes weighed enough to make two TCs. "I don't think..."

"Excuse me?"

Flo jerked around in surprise. A young woman stood outside in the hallway, a rosy cheeked toddler's tiny hand clasped in hers. "We need to get inside."

"I'm sorry, this restroom is out of order."

The toddler grabbed himself and started hopping up and down. "Mommy I gotta pee and poop!"

Flo had a Deja vu moment, except she was seeing Agnes instead of the child. "I'm really sorry."

The mother looked desperate. "He's going to soil himself."

Flo skimmed a look inside the restroom just in time to see Agnes with one knee on the counter and TC red faced and leaning as far back as she could to offset Agnes' weight. A loud creak sounded and TC jumped, nearly getting pulled over the edge of the counter as she lost focus.

"Please!" The desperate young mother said.

Flo felt a tiny hand on her thigh and looked down to find the resourceful toddler shoving past her into the bathroom. "Hey!"

She turned toward the child and the mother shot past, skidding to a stop when she spotted Agnes and TC. The two women were balanced on the edge of the counter, faces red and sweaty, and muscles jumping from the strain. TC's sneaker was resting against Agnes' well-padded chest and she was growling.

"TC, what are you doing? You're supposed to be helping her up, not shoving her down."

A vein stood out on TC's slender throat. "It's every man for himself," she ground out. "She's going to pull me off this thing and she won't let go."

"If I'm going down, so are you, sister."

The young mother sucked air, her shocked gaze riveted on the circus act playing out before her.

Flo realized she would have to abandon her spot at the door and help.

Since she'd let two people inside within five minutes she pretty much stunk at guarding the door anyway. "Hold on, TC."

Flo ran over and got underneath Agnes, shoving her wide boohind with two hands.

It was like a flea trying to propel a buffalo.

Agnes didn't budge.

Flo felt her face turning red. "You need to stop pushing her away, TC."

"I did," her friend groaned.

A slim form was suddenly pressed against Flo. She looked over to see the other woman taking up a position beside her. The young mother turned and put her back to Agnes's backside and braced her legs. "On three," she told them. "One, two, threeeeeee!" Flo and the woman pushed with everything they had. TC tugged hard, giving off an enormous grunt.

Nothing happened for a beat and then Agnes finally shifted upward. She stumbled forward and slammed into TC, smashing her into the wall.

"Oomph!" TC grunted.

Agnes pushed off the wall and straightened, scrubbing her forearm over her sweaty brow. "Well, that was exciting."

TC rubbed her boobs. "I'm pretty sure my breast tissue's trapped between my ribs."

Agnes chuckled. "Come on, let's get you into that vent before someone comes..."

Flo cleared her throat, throwing a meaningful look at the young mother.

"Comes and wants to use the sinks," Agnes said with a smile toward the woman. "We'll just make this repair and get out of your way."

"Thank you so much for your help, hun," Flo told her.

The woman shrugged. "They really should have given you a ladder."

"I know, right?" Flo said, shaking her head.

TC had the vent cover off within seconds and handed it down to Agnes. Then she stuck her head and arms inside and looked both ways. "I see light not too far away."

Agnes cupped her hands. "Put your foot into my hands and I'll heft you up."

TC did as Agnes asked and soon found herself flying upward with way too much momentum. She gave a little squeal and smashed into the wall, barely grabbing hold of the edge of the vent before oozing back down the wall like a grease spot. "Agnes, I swear I'm gonna..."

"Sorry! I forgot how skinny you are." Agnes said, grimacing. "I have shoes that weigh more than you."

"Stop talking!" TC pulled herself into the vent and slowly disappeared. They could hear her thumping through the ventilation system.

A loud creaking sound made Flo and the woman go very still, their gazes sliding toward the counter. Agnes looked down.

The counter shifted and Agnes scrambled to keep her balance, her hands slapping against the wall.

Another horrendous creak had Flo screaming. "Agnes! Come down from there!"

But Agnes couldn't move that fast. The counter canted sideways, throwing chunks of subway tiles and drywall into the air, and then ripped away from the wall and crashed downward. Agnes flew through the air, arms flailing and mouth open in a silent scream, and hit the ground hard. She tucked and rolled, crashing up against the metal door of a stall with a drawn-out groan.

Water sprayed away from the wall, courtesy of a line of broken pipes, and Flo danced backward to avoid being doused.

Behind them, a toilet flushed and the door slammed back on its hinges. The toddler came out, hands in the air and eyes wide. "Mommy, I need to wash my hands."

Flo met the woman's horrified glance. "I'm so sorry. He can probably use the sink in the men's room."

The woman marched over and grabbed her son's hand, yanking him toward the door. "This place really needs to hire more experienced janitors. You people suck."

The kid bobbed his blond head. "You suck," he mimicked before his mother dragged him through the door and let it slam closed behind her. "I told you it was out of service," Flo murmured unhappily. "Come on, Agnes. We need to get out of here before someone comes to see what happened."

Agnes shoved to her feet and lumbered toward Flo. "I think I broke my sacroiliac."

Flo pushed her toward the door. "Your sacroiliac is fine. But unless you want it checked out by prison doctors, we need to get a move on."

They shoved through the door and took a quick right turn as voices exploded from an office down the hallway. They hurried away from the footsteps pounding in their direction and ducked into the first hallway they saw, trying to look inconspicuous as more doors opened and curious people flooded out of offices.

Several moments later, Flo's pulse picked up as she remembered. "Boogers! We left TC in the vent!"

Agnes grimaced, reaching into her pocket and pulling something out. "It's worse than that. I forgot to give her the phone. She can't take any pictures."

"Come on!" Flo hurried back down the hall and toward the bathroom they'd devastated. She prayed they wouldn't run into the angry mother and her toddler, for fear they'd out them to the angry mob eying the damage. They were lucky on that score...but pretty much not on any other. There was no sign of TC in the bathroom. But there was lots of water. It covered the floor in ever-deepening pools that swirled outward, threatening to spill into the halls.

Dozens of people stood outside the room, trying to see inside.

"What in the world happened in there?" one woman asked her companion.

Said companion shrugged. "It looks like a bomb went off."

Flo tried to see past all the gawkers to find TC, but she was too short. She gave Agnes a shove. "Get up there and see if TC's shown up."

Agnes ambled through the crowd, carving a channel for herself by flinging her wide backside into people. Standing at the back, Flo could see people shooting sideways and hear the indignant exclamations as they were boohind bumped to clear a path. Agnes kept her gaze forward, to all appearances oblivious to the carnage in her wake. She reached the door and looked inside, her gaze directed much higher than everyone else's. After a moment she turned back to Flo and gave her head a single shake.

Flo wrung her hands. "Poor, TC..." Guilt swept her. TC had been dragged into her current predicament kicking and screaming. She'd known it was a situation fraught with opportunities for something to go wrong. And, true to her worst fears, she was stuck in the building's ventilation system, with nowhere to go. Flo realized her friend wouldn't want to show herself because she'd be blamed for everything that happened in the restroom. But she'd have to come out eventually.

She heard a clicking sound and turned to find Agnes playing with TC's phone. "Stop messing around, fool! We have a dire emergency." Flo suddenly realized what they needed to do. She motioned for Agnes to return and quickly came up with a plan.

A few minutes later Flo was pulling the door open to *Nightowl, Inc.* The woman behind the appointment window yanked her earbuds free and looked up as they came inside. She gave them an insincere smile. "Hello, ladies. Have you come for a rental?"

Flo had to think about that question for a moment, to figure out a way around it. "Um...yes. We have. But first, I was wondering if I could use your ladies room."

The woman nodded. "It's just outside in the hallway."

"Oh, that one's out of order," Agnes told her. "It looks like a bomb went off in there." Agnes pointed to the woman's earbuds. "You probably didn't hear it because you were listening to music or something on those."

The woman's eyes went wide and she glanced toward the door. "Really? Oh my. Should we evacuate?"

Agnes shrugged. "Maybe you should. There's water flooding out into the hall."

The woman surged to her feet. "I should check."

Flo nodded. "We'll just wait here. Let us know if we need to come back another time."

The woman barely seemed to hear them, she was hurrying out of the office like her hair was on fire.

As soon as she left, Flo hurried over and turned the lock on the door. "Come on, we need to figure out where TC is."

Agnes went into the receptionist's office and Flo headed into the first room in the short hallway leading to the back of the office. She pulled the door open and looked inside. It was a coat closet and there were no vents that she could see. She quickly closed the door and hit the next room. The room held a copier with a large shredder next to it, several boxes of paper, a box of rental signs and not much else. There was a small vent in the ceiling. Flo was pretty sure it led to a different ventilation system but she didn't really know much about how that worked so she stood below it and called TC's name anyway. She was met with silence.

When she left the storage room she saw Agnes in the room across the hall. It appeared to be a small conference room. Agnes was standing on a chair, peering into a vent on the wall. "TC?" she whispered harshly into the vent.

Flo stopped in the doorway. "Anything?"

Agnes shook her head. "You?"

"Not yet. Come on, there are three more doors to check out."

The doorknob at the front of the office turned and then stopped. Flo's eyes went wide. "Hurry up. She's back."

"Hello?" For the moment, the receptionist sounded more confused than alarmed. Flo figured that wouldn't last long.

She reached for the knob of the next door and stopped as she heard a male voice on the other side. Her eyes went wide.

"Let's go, Flo, that woman's not going to hang out there all day." Agnes' voice might as well have been an explosion in a monastery. It felt loud enough to wake the dead. Flo twitched with alarm and put her ear to the door. The voices inside had stopped. She grabbed Agnes's arm and tugged. "Hurry, they're coming."

The pounding on the outside door was getting louder. "Let me in right now! What are you two up to?" The woman was no longer confused. In fact, she'd ricocheted right past confused into enraged in a single heartbeat.

"What are you doing?" Agnes asked, her whisper nearly as loud as her regular voice. Flo shoved her into the storage room and barely got inside behind her before the door down the hallway opened and a male voice called out. "Who's out here?"

Flo's eyes went wide. Behind her, Agnes yelped softly in surprise. Flo slammed a hand over her friend's mouth. "Quiet, fool! He'll hear you," she whispered.

The soft thump of footsteps came toward them down the hall. "What's going on out here?" another male voice asked.

"I don't know," said the first man. "But I'm going to find out."

"Let! Me! In!" screamed the receptionist, followed by some truly enraged pounding on the door.

A moment later the door was opened, letting the low roar of voices from the hallway into the office. "What in the world is going on, Pamela?"

"I wish I knew, sir. I was catching up on my filing when two women came into the office and told me a bomb went off in the Ladies restroom..."

"A bomb?" Something about the second man's voice was making Flo's stomach twist with nerves. She had no idea why, but it had her heart pounding hard against her ribs.

"Wait, two women?" the first man said. "Describe them to me."

The high-pitched trill of the office phone drew the receptionist away with a murmured apology.

Flo cracked the door and risked a glance into the front office. The two men stood together in front of the door, their heads bowed as they spoke rapidly. Flo recognized the taller of the two immediately. The other one had his back turned to her and she couldn't identify him. Still, there was something about him that brought Deja vu slamming into her, nearly buckling her knees. Agnes shoved Flo gently aside. "Let me do my job."

Flo was so discombobulated it took her a minute to realize what Agnes was about to do. When she did, she opened her mouth to tell her to be careful. The words never had a chance to escape.

There was a distinct clicking noise and Agnes jumped backward with a yelp, her eyes round as she dropped TC's cell phone to the floor. The black rectangle hit the thin carpet on one corner and bounced, clanking loudly against the door. Flo stared at it, shocked into inaction. There was an ominous silence in the outer office that told Flo they were about to be discovered. If she reached for the phone...

"I knew it was you two!"

Flo scanned an unhappy look upward and grimaced at the narrowed hazel gaze boring into her. She forced a smile, lifting her hand and wiggling her fingers at the incensed man standing in front of her. "I believe you were told to stay away from this place."

Agnes shook her head. "Were we? I don't remember hearing that, did you hear that, Flo?"

She swallowed hard. If she agreed with Agnes to save her own butt, they'd put TC's narrow derriere in the wringer. She just couldn't do that to her friend.

"There you are! I can't believe you gave me the slip."

Flo couldn't credit her own eyes as TC came around the corner and peered past Detective Peters to glare at them. "TC...how..."

"I'm really mad at you two. I told you not to come in here and yet, here you are. I don't know if we can be friends anymore." TC crossed her shapely arms over her chest and glared at Flo and Agnes. "Brent, do you think you could give me a ride back to Silver Hills? I'm not getting into the car with these two, rascals. They've disrespected me for the last time."

Flo's heart twisted painfully and she suddenly found it hard to breathe. She couldn't deny that she and Agnes deserved a dressing down from TC. But the idea that their friend would never talk to them again was just too painful to endure. "TC, hun, I'm so sorr..."

"Save it, Flo!" She looked at Peters and he wrapped an arm around her shoulders.

"Of course, I'll give you a ride." He started to walk with her down the hall and then seemed to remember that he was about to leave the fox in the hen house. He stopped and turned back. "Come on, ladies."

TC clutched his arm, looking a bit desperate. "I just can't, Brent. Please don't make them come with us. I don't even want to look at them right now."

Tears flooded Flo's eyes and she sniffed. "Go ahead, hun. We'll be right behind you, I promise."

He lifted a brow in silent warning and then led his teary-eyed girlfriend out of the office. Flo nearly collapsed where she stood. She was beyond shocked at how angry TC was. She never thought she'd see the day when her friend would reject them so thoroughly.

Though she certainly couldn't blame her.

The only thing that could have shocked her worse was the sound of Agnes chuckling.

Flo whipped around in surprise, a frown forming on her face. "I can't believe you're laughing."

Agnes shook her head. "You don't actually believe that, do you?"

"Well, I..."

Agnes bent down and picked up TC's phone. "She's not really mad at us."

"I think you're wrong, Agnes."

Her friend started out of the door ahead of her. "Not a chance. That was all an act to get the detective out of here."

Flo shook her head. "I think we've gone too far this time."

"I'm right about this, Flo. You'll see."

Movement caught the corner of Flo's eye and she turned slowly, so upset she really didn't even care about the investigation anymore.

Until she saw what had caught her eye. Then she gasped. "You!"

CHAPTER TWELVE

VLAD NEWSOME WENT COMPLETELY still, blinking rapidly. "What are you two doing here?"

Flo gave him a look. "That's exactly what I was going to ask you."

"That's none of your business."

"Oh, but I think it is. You're involved with *Nightowl, Inc.* Aren't you?"

Vlad made a noncommittal sound and glanced toward the door as if considering making a run for it. He scoured a hostile gaze toward Agnes, skimming it to the phone in her hand. "What are you doing with that? You can't take pictures here without permission. Give me that!" He grabbed the phone from her hand and looked at it, giving a yelp of fear and jumping backward. The phone dropped to the floor again and landed face up.

Flo flinched as she saw the image staring back at her from the screen. The face was a mottled gray color, lumpy and wide with a large, bulbous nose and cracked lips that formed in a surprised "O". The eyes were wide and glassy, filled with terror.

Agnes sighed, snatching up the phone. "I really don't see the appeal of Facetime. Clearly you need to wear a LOT of makeup when you use it, or you look like something from the prison system."

Flo placed a hand over her heart, willing it to slow. "Wow, remind me never to press whatever button you pressed to get that."

Agnes nodded enthusiastically.

"Let me repeat my question," Vlad said snottily. "Why are you here?"

"We're trying to figure out who killed Melody and Melissa Tyne."

Vlad blinked slowly, the coolness of whatever blood he had in his veins giving him a reptilian air. "They're *both* dead?"

Flo frowned. "You knew that."

He shook his head, one pale hand reaching out to a nearby chair as if to steady himself. "I had no idea..." He fixed Flo with a perplexed look. "The mother too?"

For the first time since they'd begun investigating the deaths, Flo realized Vlad might actually be innocent. He seemed genuinely surprised. "You really didn't know about Melissa Tyne?"

Vlad stared into space for a moment and then drew himself up to his full height. The haughty look of disdain he customarily wore returned and he looked down his long nose at Flo. "If you think I had anything to do with that..."

"They were suing *Nightowl, Inc.* You have a perfect motive."

Vlad shook his head. "I was making changes. Things were going to improve. I'd spoken to the mother about it myself. She promised to drop the suit if I made...reparations."

"You admit you're part of this...?" Flo swung a hand around the *Nightowl, Inc.* office.

"Yes, of course. It's a little hard to deny when I'm standing here."

"And yet you tried," Agnes responded with an arched brow.

He looked at her as if she was something brown and aromatic on the bottom of his shoe. His thin lips curled. "I've gone to great lengths to keep my association here quiet. Why would I tell you fools and risk having it blasted around Silver Hills?"

"Why hide the fact that you're part of the company?" Flo asked. She was genuinely curious.

Vlad sighed. "It's no secret that *Nightowl* has been less than...responsive...to its clients' demands."

"People living in squalor. Infestation. No heat in the winter, no air conditioning in the deadly heat of the summer. That's one way to put it," Flo said on a frown.

"But we were working on fixing our image," he continued as if she hadn't spoken.

"Your image," Flo shook her head. "You don't care about the people living in your rentals at all, do you? You're only worried about being sued."

He shrugged. "I'll admit I can be a bit cold..."

"Ya think?" Agnes asked, clearly disgusted.

"But I can promise you I'm no murderer."

"You met with Melissa Tyne?"

"Yes. A few times."

"In her home?"

He opened his mouth to respond and then frowned, slamming it shut.

Flo had made her point and he didn't like it much. "You have motive, opportunity, and a reputation that makes it clear you aren't the most charitable human being..."

Vlad swiped a hand over his moist brow. "When you say it like that." His gaze swung to hers and something Flo had never seen entered the black depths. "I need your help."

Agnes blew a raspberry. "Fat chance, vamp."

His head whipped around so fast Flo flinched, visualizing pea soup spewing through the air. "I will drain you so dry your ancestors will turn crispy."

Agnes' eyes went wide and she gulped. "You have a funny way of asking for help."

He looked away, his manner changing on a dime. "I'm innocent. You have to help me."

Flo thought about it for a minute and then smiled as a thought occurred to her. "Fine."

He straightened, his face lighting with hope. "Really?"

"Sure," she said. "For a price. Well, two actually."

He deflated again. "Shaken down by two snoopy biddies. Okay, what's the price?"

"First, Agnes' application has to be strongly considered. If she isn't chosen for a finalist I'm going to go to Richard and have him investigate why."

Vlad's thin upper lip curled upward like a carrot sliver beneath a peeler. "Fine."

"And you have to call me by my real name from now on."

He went rigid, his pale, skinny body as taut as a bow string. Flo watched as his mouth twitched manically, clearly trying to force itself to say the words. Finally, he closed his eyes, took a deep breath and said, "Fine."

"What?"

His eyes shot open. "I said fine. I'll use your real name."

Flo let her smile widen. "Which is?"

His hands clenched into fists at his side. For a moment Flo thought he would refuse. He stood there vibrating like china in an earthquake. But then he said. "Mrs. Florence Bee."

She nodded. "Good. My friends call me Flo."

He sucked air into lungs that had probably died, unused in his narrow chest, decades earlier.

"Which is why you'll call me Mrs. Bee."

A low, rumbling sound drifted toward them and Flo realized he was growling. "Now off with you. I'll find you later to get more information about your involvement here. I have some unfinished business to attend to first."

He turned on his heel and glided quickly to the door, disappearing into the hallway faster than Flo could say "here come the pitchforks".

Agnes chuckled, lifting her big paw into the air. "High five."

Flo slapped her palm and the two of them took a pleasant moment to enjoy the win. Then Flo remembered the unfinished business she'd referred to and deflated. "We need to find TC and talk to her. I hate that she's mad at us."

They headed for the door. "She's not mad, Flo," Agnes insisted.

Flo just shook her head. Agnes was a kind and loyal woman. But her instincts and self-awareness were sometimes off when it came to her interactions with others. Flo knew that Trisha Colombo was mad and she worried her friend was angry enough to affect their friendship for the distant future.

That was unacceptable. Flo had to make it right.

If only she knew how.

WHEN THEY OPENED THE door and entered Silver Hills, they stepped into a circus-like atmosphere that seemed to have drawn most of the residents to the lobby. Well over a hundred people were milling around the entryway and Flo had a feeling their presence had something to do with the unmarked cop car sitting in the driveway outside. She spotted Roger in the crowd and headed for him. With his height and dynamic personality, he was always easy to see. Even in a crowd. At five feet three inches on a good day, Flo was just the opposite. In fact, she was like a stick bobbing on the surface of a raging river during a storm, in constant danger of getting sucked into the whirlwind and lost forever. Fortunately for her, Agnes was a huge, waterlogged tree. She wasn't going anywhere she didn't want to go.

When Flo had been shoved to the side for about the dozenth time, she got mad. "Agnes!"

Her friend turned around, frowning toward the area where Flo had been, and then reached into the melee and wrapped a massive hand around Flo's arm, yanking her through the crowd. "Stay close," Agnes yelled over the din. "Somebody must have declared Mardi Gras at Silver Hills."

She wasn't wrong. As Flo was towed through the mob, safe in Agnes' very wide wake, she noted the scent of alcohol on more than one person's breath and a wild gleam in many of their eyes.

"Doll!" She looked up to find Roger waving at them and she poked Agnes in the back.

"I see him," her friend groused as she headed in his direction.

Roger wrapped a long arm protectively around her shoulders. "Come on. Let's get out of here."

Flo tried to talk to him but her words were sucked away in the melee so she waited until he pulled her out of the crowd and into a small niche with a comfortable couch and a large screen television. "What in the world is going on?"

Agnes spurted out of the crowd behind them, bodies toppling sideways on the path behind her.

Flo spotted several people she knew in the crowd but nobody caught her eye. They were all staring at the office door, their eyes bright with anticipation.

Roger shook his head, looking grim. "I'm afraid the police showed up a few minutes ago and 'encouraged' Vlad and Morty to retreat into the office with them. I called Richard and told him he'd better get down here."

Flo felt her eyes go wide. "You think they're going to be arrested?"

He sighed. "I think it's a very good possibility."

"For the murders?" Flo asked. When Roger's expression hardened into lawyer face, she had her answer. "Oh Roger, I dislike Vlad as much as the next person, but surely they can't believe he'd kill those women."

"It doesn't matter what they think, doll. It matters what the evidence tells them." He frowned down at her, reaching out to smooth one spot on her bouff where Flo had felt someone's elbow connect. "Where have you two been anyway?"

"We went to *Nightowl, Inc.*"

Roger's expression turned angry. "Have you lost your mind? There's a very good possibility somebody at that company is behind these murders. What in the world were you thinking?"

She frowned right back at him. "I was thinking I needed to find out who was running that company."

"Detective Peters knew we were there. He sent TC to keep us out of trouble."

Roger paled. "Has he lost his mind too? That poor young woman." He stopped suddenly, looking around with a worried expression. "Where is she? Is she all right?"

Irritation bloomed at his words. Flo shoved a wave of guilt away at the memory of TC stuck in the ventilation system and pulled herself to her full height. She needn't have bothered. She barely reached his shoulder. "I can't believe you think I'd let anything happen to that young woman..."

Behind her, Agnes started to choke. Flo reached back and pinched her friend's leg.

"Ow!"

"Now doll, I didn't say..."

Flo shook her head. "Save it, Richard. I have to go speak to TC. Then we need to figure out how to help Vlad and Morty." She started to turn and then stopped, remembering the errand Roger had taken on for her earlier. "Did you find out who else is on that class action suit?"

"I did. It's a rather long list, I'm afraid."

Flo sighed, suddenly feeling overwhelmed. "Okay, can you do me a favor?"

"Of course, doll."

"Can you get that list to Detective Peters? If he's already thought about it, fine. But if he hasn't, maybe we've saved him some legwork."

Roger looked confused. "I thought you wanted his information."

"I do. But we don't have the manpower to notify that many people. Peters does. And I promised I'd share information with him so this should mollify him a bit."

"Good plan," Roger said, nodding. "I'll email it to him as soon as I get upstairs."

"Thanks, hun." Flo gave him a smile and headed down the hallway toward TC's office. She would need to apologize to him later. He wasn't wrong and she'd been defensive. She gave a long-suffering sigh, realizing she had a lot of people to make things up to. The list kept growing. Flo tried the doorknob and found it locked. She knocked but TC didn't respond.

"Let me try," Agnes said, reaching over Flo's head and knocking several times, much harder and louder. They waited a beat but TC didn't unlock the door.

"Come on, TC, open up," Flo pleaded. "We need to talk."

Nothing.

Flo thought for a moment and then pulled out her cell phone. She dialed TC's number and waited.

A ringtone sounded next to her. She looked at Agnes. Agnes looked down at the pocket of her jeans. She reached into the pocket and pulled TC's phone out. "Oh, oh."

"Satan's boogers!" Flo exclaimed. "We've made a total mess of this, haven't we?"

CHAPTER THIRTEEN

THEY ARRIVED BACK AT the lobby just in time to see Vlad being escorted out of the building in handcuffs. Detective Peters caught Flo's eye at the door and frowned, giving his head a quick shake when she started forward. She forced herself to hang back, knowing that she couldn't do anything to stop them from taking Vlad in. But she fully intended to visit the station later to try to talk some sense into the young cop.

Or at the very least find out what evidence he possessed that had inspired the arrest.

The crowd's attention was drawn to the office door, where a lone figure stood, her dark gaze filled with menace. Flo felt a chill as those dark eyes found hers and shivered.

"He didn't take Morty," Agnes said in Flo's ear.

"No. He didn't." Flo held the woman's gaze and nodded. She turned to Agnes. "Come on." Flo figured Vlad must have insisted Morty had nothing to do with *Nightowl* or the murders. The fact that she hadn't been hauled away in handcuffs told Flo that Peters must have believed him. Although he had to be aware that she was seen at Melody Tyne's home at the time of the murder. Morty turned and went back into the office without addressing the crowd. Flo half expected the door to be locked, but when she turned the knob it opened. Morty was standing across the room in front of the window, staring out into the gathering darkness. She stood straight and still, barely even breathing.

Even from across the room Flo could feel her rage vibrating on the air.

"Lock it," Morty said in a deep, throaty growl.

Flo and Agnes shared a look and then Agnes reached out and turned the deadbolt on the door.

They stood in silence for a long moment, each one waiting for the other to speak first. Finally, Morty turned away from the window. Her narrow face was taut with rage, her blood-red lips pinched. The hard planes of her face made her look like she'd been chiseled from pale marble and her eyes were dark pools of menace. But when she spoke, the words, if not her tone, were touched with humor. "Kind of like Deja vu, isn't it?"

Flo didn't want to smile. It didn't seem right under the circumstances. But she tilted her head downward in acknowledgment of Morty's little joke. It was exactly like Deja vu. Only the last time a Newsome had been taken from Silver Hills in cuffs it had been Morty herself. "We're going to help clear his name," Flo told the other woman.

Morty didn't acknowledge Flo's statement in any way. She simply stood there, hands crossed in front of her, and stared at them. Finally, she gave a tiny sigh and nodded. "Thank you."

"Of course. Vlad has his faults, but he's not a killer."

Morty frowned as if she wasn't sure Flo was right. Her reaction didn't exactly warm the cockles of Flo's heart. "He *is* innocent, right?"

Morty's smooth, pale brow furrowed. "Of course, he is."

Flo nodded. "Good. Now tell us what in the world is going on so we can help you."

Morty stood stiffly before them, her jaw tight. For a long moment Flo didn't think she was going to respond. But then she inclined her chin, staring at a spot on the floor between them. "It's no secret we have rental properties that are...substandard...in some small ways."

It was Flo's turn to frown. But she held her tongue, figuring that antagonizing the woman wouldn't get her what she needed.

"But we've been trying to fix that. We've seen the error of our ways and have been working to correct the problem." Her gaze rolled up to Flo as if to assess how her story was being accepted.

"Go on," Flo said.

"We've hired new managers for all the buildings and set aside funds for repairs and updating." She shook her head. "We've been working with a business consultant to turn things around."

"That's good. But let's start at the beginning. Do you and Vlad own *Nightowl, Inc.*?"

She sighed. "Yes."

"Okay. So you lied to my face..." Flo held up a hand to stop Morty from responding. "Moving on...you're trying to fix things at the rentals. I applaud that. But the Tynes must not have been happy about your efforts because they started a class action suit against you."

"They launched that suit before we started fixing things up. To be honest, it was the final nail in the coffin for us..." Her gaze lifted again and a tight smile played across her lips. "So to speak."

Agnes chuckled darkly.

"That's why Vlad...and you...went to their homes. To try to talk them into reconsidering their suit under your new business model," Flo asked.

She nodded. "We promised them free rent for a year and committed to addressing each and every concern of all the plaintiffs in that suit."

"But they weren't biting?"

"They wouldn't even listen." She fixed Flo with a dark, hostile gaze. "That lawsuit would have ruined us."

"You realize you're giving me a powerful motive for murder."

Morty turned back to the window. "I do. But I can promise you we would never kill anyone. We were even negotiating a deal with *Rest Easy Security* to give all our renters security systems at a reduced rate." She turned back, her expression suddenly earnest. "We were trying to protect them."

Flo realized that must be the name of Buddy Parks' new business. "Because of all the recent break-ins?"

"Yes."

"Do you know who owns that security company?"

"Mr. Buddrick? I haven't met him personally but we've communicated by email several times. He's offering us a great price for bulk sales. I understand he's trying to get his business off the ground."

"His real name is Buddy Parks. He was the founder of the *White Light Kindredship.*"

Morty's eyes went wide. "That cult you two took down a while back?"

"That's the one."

Morty lifted her hands to her face and covered her mouth, her dark eyes glistening. It was the most human gesture Flo had ever seen the other woman make and it almost made her feel sorry for Morty.

Almost.

"Vlad's going to prison."

"Not if we have anything to say about it, hun. Roger Attles is helping us and we're going to get to the bottom of these murders." And if Vlad was guilty, Flo thought, so be it. But if he was innocent, she wanted to make sure he didn't pay for someone else's crime. Particularly Buddy Parks'. "Given that Parks is involved, it's a pretty good bet he's the killer. Now we just need to prove it."

Morty nodded. "Okay. How can I help?"

"By not letting Parks know you suspect anything. You'll be on the inside of this and we'll need you to feed us everything you get from Parks."

"I can do that."

"Also..." Flo wasn't sure how Morty was going to take the next request, but it was important. "Agnes and I want to rent one of your apartments."

"Whatever for?"

"You'll just have to trust me on this one, Morty. It's the only way I can think of to get to the bottom of what's going on."

Morty thought about the request for a moment and then agreed. "Okay. But you have to promise me you won't join the class action suit against us."

"Ha, ha," Flo said.

THE NEXT MORNING, FLO was really glad she hadn't promised not to join the suit. After walking through the "apartment" Morty had agreed to rent them, she was thinking she might need to bring her own suit.

Maybe a hazmat suit.

The situation was made more dire by the fact that she'd committed to living with Agnes who, though she presented the facade of being casual and unconcerned about most things, was really almost OCD in her personal life. Her friend was standing just inside the apartment door, looking around at the stained shag carpeting and the scarred walls painted a yellowed and splotched white. "Is that mold over there?" Agnes asked with a shudder.

Flo turned to the area in question, grimacing. There was an irregularly shaped, dark gray spot on the wall between the baseboard and the window, like an inkblot of death. "That would be my guess." Flo's gaze scanned upward from the spot, to the ancient window air conditioner. The unit dripped steadily onto the carpet, groaning and gasping as it attempted to keep up with the mild temperatures beyond the glass. Flo realized the air conditioner would be worse than useless on a truly hot day.

"I can feel my sinuses cramping," Agnes told her. "My chest feels tight."

Flo rolled her eyes. "Buck up soldier. Just think of this as another stake out."

Agnes looked appalled. "You don't actually expect me to eat in here?"

Flo couldn't believe what she was hearing. She'd actually found a situation where Agnes couldn't eat. She couldn't wait to tell the others. That thought brought despair dancing upon its heels. Flo knew that as soon as Roger and the others found out what she had planned there would be hell to pay. They would never support her and Agnes using themselves as bait. The thought made Flo's chest a little tight too. But then she consoled herself with the knowledge that all the break-ins had been done while the inhabitants of the apartments were away. She and Agnes should be perfectly safe.

"Couldn't we get a place that was a little less..." Agnes appeared to be struggling for a descriptive word that properly captured the essence of the apartment. "—uninhabitable?"

Flo walked over and eyed the sagging couch in the middle of the room. It was a putrid shade of green and was shaped like the back of a forty-year-old horse. Flo was pretty sure if she pressed her hand against the cushion in the center something would bite her through the crusty fabric. There were probably mice or squirrels living in the thing. Happily, she had no plans to touch it...or anything else in the apartment. "We needed to be in the building that's had the most break-ins. With any luck we'll only be in here for one night."

Agnes's eyes went wide. "I can't sleep here. I'll die."

Flo wanted to scold her friend for being melodramatic, but with the mold and bacteria level in the place, she wasn't entirely sure Agnes was wrong. "I brought us a tent. We'll pitch it in one of the bedrooms and sleep on an air mattress with the flaps zipped up. That way the rats can't get to us." Flo became aware of a wobbly quality in her voice as she tried to reassure Agnes. Since her friend didn't look at all convinced, she figured Agnes noticed it too.

"How long do we need to stay in here before we go out again?"

Flo looked at her watch. "I suppose it would be okay if we went out to lunch."

"Thank god!" Agnes said, turning back to the door.

"But it's only ten o'clock," Flo said quickly.

"I don't care. I'm fine with eating lunch early."

Flo sighed. "Just wait a minute. I need to try TC again."

"You still haven't talked to her?"

"No," Flo answered. "And I'm starting to get worried." She listened to TC's office phone ring on the other end and then left a quick message. "It's me again, TC. Please call me back. I want to apologize. I don't like having you mad at me." Flo disconnected and stood there frowning.

"Maybe she's not in the office."

Flo really wished they hadn't accidentally kept TC's cell phone. "Well we can't get hold of her any other way. We'll just have to wait until she goes in or calls to get her messages. Richard said she didn't even ask him for the day off. She just didn't show up." Flo shook her head. "No matter how mad she is at us, she wouldn't skip out on work. Richard's worried too."

"Maybe we should go to the station and tell Detective Peters," Agnes said hopefully.

"No. We can't be seen going to the station. Just in case..." She tapped her foot on the nasty carpet and then immediately regretted it as a cloud of dust and a stomach-churning musty odor wafted upward. She sneezed violently several times.

When she'd gotten her nose under control, Flo waved a hand toward the door. "Let's go. We can stop at the drug store to stock up on antihistamines before we get lunch."

She didn't have to ask Agnes twice. Her friend was out the door and bolting up the sidewalk to Flo's car before Flo even made it outside.

CHAPTER FOURTEEN

THE DINER ON MAIN STREET was already hopping when Flo and Agnes arrived at eleven. It had taken them forever to stock up on all the items Agnes thought she needed if she was going to spend one night in the apartment. To Flo's shock, none of it included food. If she refused to eat in the apartment, Agnes would have to eat a lot at the diner to get her through the hours before they went out to dinner and ate again.

Flo waved at a couple of people she knew and then followed Agnes' wide boohind through the diner, to a booth at the back. Agnes liked to sit back there because she could see what everybody was eating and decide what looked good before she ordered. She slipped into the side of the booth facing the restaurant and Flo took the other side. She opened her menu and perused the offerings, deciding on soup and salad before closing it again and looking around. Spotting several familiar faces across the room, Flo waved and smiled. "The Baccarat brothers are here too," she said. Bill lifted a hand and gave her a half-hearted wave before reapplying himself to his lunch. His brothers ignored her entirely.

"I still can't believe Vlad the Repeller and the world's most unfriendly triplets had a friendly conversation on the street the other day."

Agnes was scanning the plates around them, clearly still trying to figure out what to eat. "I still say there's something going on there. Maybe he paid them to vote for his choice of manager."

"I wouldn't put it past him." Flo eyed the brothers quizzically, wondering if they could be swayed by money. They didn't seem to have a lot of money, though Flo realized they were always dressed well and they drove an expensive, foreign-made car. They were apparently doing okay. "What do they do for a living?" She asked Agnes.

Agnes shrugged. "I thought one of them was an accountant and one of them might be a snake handler or some kind of religious leader. I'm not really sure. I think Bo's a doctor or something."

"I should talk to Eliza Kemp when we get back to Silver Hills. I'll bet she knows."

Agnes closed her menu as the waitress hurried by laden with food and promised she'd be right back to take their order. "Why do you care?"

"I'm not sure. I guess I just want to know what motivates them. I'm pretty sure Vlad didn't kill anybody, but you and I both know he's up to something."

"Maybe he's running for Mayor," Agnes said on a grin.

Flo flinched. "Bite your tongue."

"What can I get you, ladies?" The careworn face of the waitress split in a grin. "Besides pie."

Agnes grinned widely. "The peach pie looks delicious."

"Oh, it is." The woman scrawled on her order pad. "What else?"

"I'll have the turkey dinner, please," Agnes told her. "With dressing, mashed potatoes and green bean casserole. I'll also take a side of coleslaw and some baked beans please. Oh, and ice cream on my pie."

The woman's eyes went wide. "My goodness, eating for two today?" She winked at Agnes.

"It has to hold me for a while," Agnes lamented.

Flo shook her head. "A bowl of vegetable soup please, and a salad with Italian dressing."

The woman nodded, jotting the order down. "Pie?"

"Oh, why not?" Flo agreed, handing her the menus. "Thanks, hun."

"My pleasure."

Agnes slipped from the booth as the waitress walked away. "I need to go scour my hands in boiling water, just in case I touched something in that death trap."

Flo sighed. "Okay." She grabbed her purse and dug into it, looking for a tissue. Somebody slipped into the seat across the booth and she looked up with a smile. The smile died a quick death and ice slipped down her spine. "What are *you* doing here?"

The man Flo knew as Buddy Parks gave her a smug smile. "Hello, Mrs. Bee. How are you?" She took note of the tidy beard adorning his once closely-shaved chin and the way his thick, dark brown hair curled just below his ears where before it had been much shorter and swept back from his face. Outwardly at least, he'd changed from the calm, serene "Bright One" of cult days. He looked more like a business man.

She frowned. "You should be in jail."

Parks shrugged, the smile never wavering. "I feel really bad about those kids." He heaved an insincere sigh. "My daughter's always been a bit off, if you know what I mean."

"The apple apparently doesn't fall far from the tree."

His eyes lost the smile even as his lips maintained it. "You're very judgmental, Mrs. Bee. It's an unattractive trait."

"Then it's a good thing I'm not trying to attract anybody." She leaned forward, angrily jabbing the table between them with a finger. "I don't know what you're up to, Mr. Parks but you stay away from me and my friends. We don't for a minute believe you're turning over a new leaf and I will call the police on you if you so much as look sideways at one of us."

He stared across the table for a long moment, all pretense at pleasantness gone. "If I should choose to 'look sideways' as you put it, you won't even see me coming. Don't presume to try to go up against me, Mrs. Bee. You won't survive the encounter." He slid smoothly from the booth. But he didn't leave right away. Pasting an insincere smile on his coldly handsome face, Buddy Parks leaned close. Flo shifted away from him but his hot breath still bathed her face. "Stay out of my business you old busybody. Or you'll regret it."

Flo's heart started pounding and she felt faint. She didn't even realize he'd left until she heard footsteps hurrying in her direction. She looked up into Bill Baccarat's worried face. "Are you okay, Mrs. Bee? You look like you're going to faint."

She reached out and clasped his hand. "That man who was just here. He threatened me."

Bill frowned, looking around the diner. "What man?"

Flo looked around too. Parks was nowhere to be seen. "You didn't see him?"

"Sorry. I just looked up from my food and saw you struggling to stay upright." He pulled out his cell phone. "Is there someone I can call for you? I don't think you should be driving in your condition."

Flo was so disappointed the man hadn't noticed Buddy Parks that it didn't even occur to her she was having an actual conversation with him. Unfortunately, he probably thought she was cray-cray. Flo shook her head, forcing a smile. "I'm here with a friend. I'll be fine. Thank you for coming over to check on me though. That was very kind."

He hesitated. "Are you sure you'll be all right?"

"I'm sure. Thank you though."

He finally nodded and returned to his table.

Flo lowered her face into her hands, fighting tears. Agnes found her that way a moment later.

"Hey? What's up? You look like you saw a ghost," Agnes asked as she slipped into the booth.

The food arrived just then so Flo held her response. But as she waited for the waitress to cover the table with all of Agnes' food, Flo couldn't help wondering if she *had* seen a ghost.

Clearly, Parks' threat hadn't been noticed by anyone else.

FLO HAD TROUBLE EATING her lunch. Her stomach roiled with nerves and telling Agnes about what had happened didn't seem to make it any better. Her friend listened and made the appropriate noises but, when Flo asked the waitress about the man who'd approached their booth and the woman seemed clearly confused by the question, even Agnes couldn't keep the doubt from her gaze. "I'm telling you he was here!" Flo frowned across the table at Agnes.

Her friend lifted her hands. "I don't doubt that he was, Flo. I'm just trying to figure out what he's up to."

Flo sighed, scrubbing a hand over her face. "I couldn't tell you. One thing I know for sure is that he's not up to what he says he's up to."

"I'm not so sure about that." Agnes held up a hand when Flo bristled. "Just hear me out. If Parks *was* trying to get the business going and he saw *Nightowl, Inc.* as his pathway to making that happen, he just might decide that stopping the suit was his best option."

Flo couldn't argue with the logic of that. "Okay, that makes sense if you're a madman."

"Which we know Parks is," Agnes said soothingly. "I'm on your side, Flo."

"I know, hun. I'm sorry I snapped at you."

"You're justified. If that man had threatened me I'd be frazzled too."

Flo couldn't stop the grin that twitched on her lips. "No, you wouldn't. You'd punch him."

Agnes chuckled. "Maybe. But even I understand that your way is better."

When Flo showed her surprise, Agnes clarified. "If we attacked him he'd take the high road. He'd become the victim. The police already believe he's turning over a new leaf. We'd play right into his hands."

"You know you're pretty smart, Miss Willard?"

"Don't sound so surprised."

"Well, you have to admit you hide it well."

They both laughed and Flo felt better. Agnes was on her side and Flo had a plan that would set them on the path of finding a killer. Things were going to be all right. "Well, I guess we'd better go back to the apartment."

Agnes' grin faded quickly. "Please don't make me."

"Don't be such a baby. This is for a good cause." Flo's phone rang and she saw with surprise that it was Detective Parks. She answered, hoping he had news of TC. "Have you heard from TC today?"

It was a measure of his concern that he didn't give her a hard time about not greeting him. "No. I was hoping you had. I'm really worried about her Flo."

Something dark moved into Flo's chest and made it hard, suddenly, to breathe. "I wasn't worried at first because I knew how angry she was at me. But it's not like her to miss work without calling in, Detective."

"I know. I'm sitting in front of her house and she's not here either. I tracked her phone and it came up at the diner downtown. I'm heading there now."

Flo grimaced. "Um..."

"What's wrong?" His voice was filled with tension. Flo was worried about what he'd do when he heard what she was about to tell him. "I'm really sorry."

"Okay, you're scaring me. Just spit it out, Flo."

"Agnes and I have TC's phone. We're at the diner."

A long, drawn-out silence met her admission. Flo could almost hear his teeth gritting through the phone line. "And how did that happen?"

"It's a long story and you wouldn't like any of it so let me just say it was an accident and I'd give almost anything if it hadn't happened."

He sighed. Flo could picture him dragging a hand over his face, frustration clear in his jerky movements. But it was the pure, animal fear she knew would be in his eyes that made her stomach twist. "I'm really sorry, hun."

"We need to find her."

"Yes. We do." Flo realized in that moment that she'd been concentrating on the wrong thing. When in all probability TC's disappearance was probably tied to the murders and the whole *Nightowl* mess. "I think I know who might have her."

"Who?"

"Buddy Parks."

"Flo..." Exasperation filled his voice.

"Hear me out! He was here. At the diner. And he threatened me. You know he has a history of kidnapping unwilling people..."

"I know his daughter does."

"Oh, take off the blinders, Detective!"

Heads turned in her direction and she flushed. She hadn't meant to scream at him. "Look, can you meet us somewhere?"

He hesitated only a moment, a clear indication of his desperation since he thought her Parks theory was all wet. "Fine. At Silver Hills?"

"No. I'll give you an address. We'll meet you there in twenty minutes."

CHAPTER FIFTEEN

DETECTIVE PETERS CLIMBED slowly out of his un-marked SUV and stood in the street, looking at the building with a frown on his face. He obviously thought he was in the wrong place.

Flo opened the front door and called out to him, motioning him inside.

His look of perplexity soon turned to one of disapproval. "Mrs. Bee. Why am I here?"

She looked around to make sure nobody noticed his arrival. "Hurry up, come inside."

He narrowed his gaze but did as she asked. "Is TC here?"

"Why would you think that?"

"Because I can't imagine any other reason you would have come to this...place."

Flo shook her head. "That's not important. We need to talk about Parks."

But he wasn't listening. He was staring at Agnes. "Why is she standing there with her hands out and her eyes closed?"

Flo rolled her eyes. "She says she's meditating."

"Standing up?"

"Don't ask," Flo told him. "Agnes! Will you join us please?"

Her friend opened one eye and gave the Detective a wary look. "I'm fine right here. I think I've come to grips with the germs in this two square foot area."

Peters chuckled, earning himself a glare from the germaphobe. "Oh. You're not joking."

"Look around, Detective. Do you *think* I'm joking?"

"Whatever." He dismissed Agnes, focusing on Flo. "If you have an idea where Trisha is, tell me now. We're wasting time. I can't shake the feeling she's in trouble."

"I already told you. Parks has her."

"Mrs. Bee, we've been over this..."

"And you refuse to see what this man is capable of. I've *seen*, Detective. More than once. You have to trust me. TC's life may depend on it."

He sighed. "Okay, tell me what happened."

Flo filled him in on her encounter with Buddy Parks at the diner.

Peters looked very unhappy when she was finished. "Did anyone else hear him threaten you?"

"No. He's too smart for that." Frustration made her frown. She knew Peters thought her feelings about Parks were coloring her opinion and she was afraid he'd dismiss her concerns because of it.

She was right. Peters shook his head. "I can't confront the man based only on your word, Flo. I'm sorry."

Flo fought tears. "You'll be *very* sorry if TC gets hurt because you're just too dang stubborn to listen."

He looked at the floor, his face flushed and his jaw tight. He was obviously angry at her. But he was also worried. And Flo hoped that would be enough to make him see reason.

"I'm not asking you to arrest Parks. Just stop by his home or place of business and see what you can see."

"If he does have TC he'll just lie about it," Peters told her, looking miserable.

"Use your instincts, Detective. You have very good ones."

He expelled air. "I guess it's worth a try." When he caught Flo's eye again his gaze was taut with fear. "TC's in trouble and I feel helpless."

She patted his arm. "Don't worry. I have a feeling this will all end tonight."

"Mrs. Bee, whatever you're planning you need to give it up. You're not equipped to deal with a murderer. Leave that to the police."

Flo shrugged. "I don't know what you're talking about. Agnes and I are just staying here while our apartments are fumigated."

He glanced toward Agnes and her friend quickly closed her eye. "Om," she chanted, her eyes squinched shut.

"I got your om," Peters muttered. He stopped at the door. "I mean it, Flo. Go home and give this up. The last thing TC would want is for you two to get hurt because of her."

"Wait!"

He stepped through the door and halted, turning back.

"Why did you arrest Vlad Newsome?"

"Because the evidence told me he's guilty."

"What evidence?"

He glowered at her. "I can't talk about an ongoing investigation, Mrs. Bee. You know that."

She did. But she'd been hoping he'd make an exception for her. "Okay, let's try this. I'll talk and you just frown if I get something wrong."

He sighed, glancing impatiently toward his car. "Make it fast."

"First of all, did you see Parks at *Nightowl* when you were there? TC spotted him going into the office."

Peters' handsome face showed his surprise before he could contain it.

"Okay, he must have slipped out before you got there." Flo nodded. "I'm guessing you found Vlad's prints in Melissa Tyne's home?"

He stared at her, his expression remaining neutral.

"You talked to him at the *Nightowl, Inc.* offices and realized his connection to the company gives him motive. It puts him at risk of losing everything if the lawsuit goes through."

Nothing.

"What I don't understand is, why didn't you arrest him at the office? Why did you wait until he got back to Silver Hills? In front of his wife and friend...erm...acquaintances?"

Peters just lifted an eyebrow.

"Ah, he slipped away while you were talking to us, didn't he?"

When she and Agnes had spotted Vlad in the office, he'd clearly just emerged from some kind of hidey hole. He'd seemed surprised to have been spotted.

"Okay, last thing. You have witnesses who can put the Newsome vehicle at Melody Tyne's home the day of the murder."

He lifted a dark gold eyebrow in surprise. "How do you...?"

She shook her head. "That's not important. Vlad didn't kill those women, Detective. I'd stake my life on it."

He turned toward the street. "I hope you don't have to, Flo."

"Everything you have is circumstantial."

He simply shrugged. If he had something more significant he wasn't going to tell her. "Stay away from Newsome and this case. Trust me to do my job for once."

Flo didn't respond. She didn't tell him what she suspected because she knew he'd only try to stop her. But she hadn't been lying to him. One way or the other she was going to see an end to the mystery and the murders that very night.

She only hoped things went as planned because Plan A was squiggy enough. Plan B was off the charts terrible.

"AGNES, YOU CAN'T KEEP all your parts off the floor at the same time."

Her friend was lying on the floor of the tent, a pillow stuffed under her butt and her shoulders propped up by her duffel bag. Her feet were resting on a box she'd found in the trunk of Flo's car. She'd doubled up on the blankets on the floor of the tent but she still seemed reluctant to put her hands down.

"You're being ridiculous. This tent has a nylon floor as a barrier."

"Germs can get through nylon."

"I really don't think so."

"There's something crunchy under there. I think it's the bones of a dead mouse."

Flo sighed. "Let's just turn off the flashlights and try to get some sleep."

"How am I supposed to sleep? It's only seven o'clock. Besides, I feel like bedbugs are crawling over my skin."

"There are no bedbugs in my tent. It was new in the box...the box you have your feet propped on as a matter of fact...before we put it up."

Agnes gave a heartfelt sigh. "I miss my cat and my bed."

"I know, hun. I miss Rodney too. But hopefully we'll be home before they even notice we're gone."

Agnes' gaze widened and she turned hopefully to Flo. "What about Rodney's dinner? And he'll need to go out for a potty break. We should go back."

"Rodney's fine. Roger's babysitting him for me."

"You told Roger what we were doing?"

"Of course not! He would have had a conniption fit. I told him we were going to a show in Indianapolis tonight and would be home late."

"You're getting very good at lying, Flo."

She sighed. Agnes was right. Flo used to at least feel guilty about lying to her friends. But it had become second nature to her.

"Tell me again why we're going to sleep so early?"

"It's just a nap because we're going to be up all night watching the apartment."

"What for?"

"We've been over this already. We're going to hide and wait for the thieves to show up. Then we're going to get pictures of them and give them to Detective Peters. My theory is that they're working for Parks and if the police squeeze them hard enough maybe they'll give him up." Flo turned to her friend, feeling slightly guilty. "It could get dangerous if they see us. I'll understand if you don't want to join me outside."

Agnes shifted on her pillow, resting her hands on her round belly before settling back with a grimace on the lumpy duffel. "I don't even care. Right now, I just want to be out of this place. Maybe we should go hide early so we're not spotted."

Flo punched her pillow up and settled onto it with a sigh. She was tired. It had been a long, stressful day. It would feel good to get a little rest before their spying started. "Just close your eyes and try to rest, hun."

Flo's phone rang. She looked at the ID and saw that it was Morty. "Hey, Morty. What's up?"

"You wanted me to give you information from Parks when I got it."

Flo sat up. "I did."

"I just spoke with him. Apparently, he's on his way out of town. He said he's heading to Chicago for a few days to talk to his distributor. I thought you'd want to know."

Flo frowned. "Do you believe him?"

"Actually, yes. I heard him talking to the toll operator while we were on the phone."

"Okay. Thanks."

Despite her weariness Flo couldn't fall asleep. Aside from wondering about Parks and his sudden trip out of town, she'd never been good at sleeping in strange places. It had taken her a month to sleep through the night when she'd first moved to Silver Hills.

To make things worse, the apartment was filled with strange sounds. Dripping and creaking and roaring...and that was just the air conditioner. Outside the wind was whipping up and Flo heard raindrops smacking against the cloudy glass of the window over their heads. It would be a cold rain. The temperatures had been dropping all day as the storm moved in. She lay there and worried about staking the apartment out in the rain.

Her eyes shot open on a terrible thought. What if the thieves took the night off because of the weather?

A long, drawn-out rumble rolled through the tent and Flo shot Agnes a look. Her friend was lying on her back, rigid as a frozen worm. Her mouth was hanging open and she was snoring like a sailor on leave.

Figures. Flo should have known better than to worry about Agnes sleeping.

A gust of wind made the glass in the window creak ominously. Flo gave up trying to sleep and sat up. She'd try to read for a while. She was digging in her small bag looking for her ereader when another, high-pitched creak had her head snapping up.

That one hadn't been the window.

Somebody was in the apartment with them!

She stilled, rigid with panic, and was afraid to move for fear that whoever it was would hear her.

Another nasally rumble pulled her nerves taut and Flo gritted her teeth. It would be impossible for the intruder to miss Agnes' snoring. She snaked a hand slowly across the distance between them and smacked Agnes on the arm. Her friend snorted several times, sounding like a buffalo running from a hunter, and then settled back to sleep, loudly smacking her lips.

Flo pinched her and Agnes jumped, her mouth coming open along with her eyes.

Flo slapped a hand over Agnes' mouth before she could complain about the pinch and pressed a finger over her own lips. She leaned close and whispered. "Somebody's in the apartment."

Agnes' eyes went wide. She nodded and Flo dropped her hand.

Another creak was followed by the unmistakable rustle of fabric.

Agnes grasped the flashlight nearest her hand and started to move.

Flo shook her head, holding up a hand to stop her.

A figure was suddenly standing in the bedroom, visible only as a wavering shadow against the thin nylon of the tent. The figure loomed over them, looking massive. Flo hoped it was an illusion. The streetlight beyond the window was painting the intruder in just enough light to outline him, while the wind in the tree beyond the glass was making him appear to move.

She reached down and grasped her own flashlight, looking at Agnes. Agnes nodded and shifted sideways so she could move past Flo when the time came. "On three," Flo whispered so softly she wasn't sure her friend would even hear. But she couldn't risk the man outside the tent hearing.

Flo held up three fingers. She dropped one and Agnes shifted forward. She dropped the second finger and Agnes lifted her hand, the flashlight extending from it. She hesitated a beat and then took a deep breath, finally dropping the third finger.

"Who's out there?" Flo screamed even as she hit the button and sent a burst of painfully bright light directly at the intruder.

Agnes burst forward and hit the door of the tent with a feral scream. Sadly, they'd forgotten it was zipped. Agnes hit the nylon and it bulged outward, smacking into the figure speared on the end of Flo's light. But Agnes couldn't reach him with her weapon because she was cocooned in nylon. That didn't mean she didn't try. She dug in with a growl and forced the tent forward, dragging Flo with her as she pulled it another inch closer.

Sadly, there was nowhere to go. When the tent stopped moving Agnes fell forward, hitting the floor with a heavy thump and a ripping sound as the zipper gave way under her weight. Flo landed on her friend's legs with a grunt.

The distant sound of the front door slamming had Flo scrambling past Agnes. "Come on, we need to catch him!"

But by the time they hit the door there was no sign of any intruder. "Dangit!" Flo exclaimed in frustration. They hadn't solved the mystery and there was no way the thieves would come back after barely getting away the first time.

"I'm sorry, Flo."

She shook her head, scraping angry tears from her cheeks. "It's not your fault. I didn't expect them so early."

Agnes frowned. "I thought the thieves only came when the people who lived there were out."

"Yeah. That's what I thought too."

"Maybe it wasn't the thieves," Agnes offered, her expression dire. "Maybe it was somebody who was hoping to catch us here."

Flo hadn't considered that. And the idea didn't make her happy. "I certainly hope not, because if you're right..."

"We were lucky not to end up like Melissa and Melody Tyne."

AGNES GAVE FLO A WEARY wave goodbye as the elevator doors closed on the second floor. Flo trudged down the quiet hallway, wondering if it was too late to get Rodney back from Roger. She'd miss sleeping with him and was worried the little dog was torturing Roger with wanting to be held and taken out for walks.

She smiled at the thought. Roger loved her annoying little dog and he was probably enjoying every minute of Rodney's shenanigans. She unlocked her door and stepped inside, enjoying the clean smell and tidiness of her own little piece of heaven. She would never take it for granted again. And she also vowed to threaten Morty and Vlad. If they didn't make those apartments right for their tenants, Flo decided she *would* join the suit against them.

Nobody should have to live like that.

She briefly considered having a shower but decided she was too tired. She'd have one first thing in the morning, before going down to breakfast. Flo washed her face and brushed her teeth and then slipped into her pajamas, trudging wearily to bed. She didn't think she even had the energy to read her book and decided to just go right to sleep. Glancing at the clock, she saw it was after midnight. No wonder she was so tired. Flo wasn't used to being up past eleven. She grabbed the top of her comforter and folded it back. As she did, something flipped up and fluttered to the floor on the other side of the bed. Flo came instantly awake, her nerves humming. Hurrying around the bed, she looked down at the small square of heavy photo paper. It was upside down so she couldn't see the image on its surface.

With a sense of dread climbing through her belly, Flo reached down and picked the photo up, turning it over.

She gasped, crying out with horror as she looked at the terrible image on the page. Her legs gave out and she dropped to the bed, her eyes captivated by the photo and the horrifying implications. After a moment she roused herself, her heart pounding in her throat as she reached for the phone. Detective Peters answered on the second ring, his voice breathless. "What is it? Have you heard from her?"

"I haven't. But I know where TC is. And it isn't good."

CHAPTER SIXTEEN

SHE'D NEVER SEEN THE young detective quite that shade of gray before. His jaw was tight and his movements were jerky. He was clearly very upset. "You said this was in your apartment?"

Flo nodded, her pulse picking up as she realized TC's abductor had been in her home. She dropped heavily onto the hard wooden chair on the other side of Detective Peters' desk. "Poor TC. I'm sure she's terrified." And she couldn't help feeling grateful Rodney hadn't been there. He would have barked at the intruder, and most likely have gone for the guy's calf. He might have been hurt. Or worse...

The picture of TC tied up and blindfolded in a chair would most likely stay with Flo for the rest of her life. She couldn't see her friend's face because it was covered by a cloth sack, but she read the terror in the droop of her head and the rigid set to her long, slender form. Flo heard the familiar click of a magazine being seated and looked up to see Peters slipping his service weapon into a shoulder holster. She realized with a flash of clarity that he was going without her. She stood up, setting her jaw and locking her gaze on his. "I'm coming too."

Peters gave one hard jerk of his head. "Not a chance, Flo."

"I know that place. Agnes and I have been inside. You have to let me come."

He grabbed a jacket off the back of his chair and pulled it on over the holster. "It's too dangerous."

Flo hurried after him as he headed for the door. "She's my friend!" The words had come out louder and more filled with desperation than Flo had intended. It was enough to stop him in his tracks. Peters turned back and nodded his head in acceptance of the sentiment. "I love her too, Mrs. Bee. I'll bring her back."

Watching him walk out of that station was the hardest thing Flo had ever done. She realized in a flash of intuition that she was a person for whom action was a balm. It was a trait that sometimes brought her within trouble's grasp. But it had served her well throughout her life. Flo frowned, clenching her fists as she fought the desire to run after him and force him to let her come. She turned to look at the phone on his desk, wondering if Agnes would answer if she called. She even went so far as to walk over and put her hand on the old-fashioned receiver.

But in the end, she resisted the urge. Barely. He was right. She was ill-prepared for what needed to be done. And if something happened to TC because she jumped when she should have stepped back...

Flo glanced up at the clock. One o'clock in the morning.

It was going to be a long, long night.

A DOOR SLAMMED SHUT and Flo jerked upward at the sound. She looked around the squad room, momentarily disoriented. She sat up with a muffled groan, reaching up to rub the throbbing pain between her eyes. Two uniformed cops walked past the desk, smiling. "Good morning, Mrs. Bee."

They didn't ask her why she'd been sleeping on Detective Peters' desk and she didn't offer any explanation. As the fog of sleep cleared, Flo realized what their being at the PD meant. Her gaze jerked up to the clock on the wall.

Seven o'clock!

She silently berated herself for having fallen asleep. The two cops disappeared down the hall and she could hear their cheerful voices and the clink of the coffee pot against their mugs. Flo jumped to her feet and hurried after them. "Have you seen Detective Peters?"

The younger of the two cops shook his head. He had tightly curled light brown hair and freckles and looked like he was about twelve. Flo couldn't remember his name. She looked to the other cop.

Officer Manchion frowned. "He doesn't usually get here for a couple of hours. Is there a problem?"

Flo thought fast. If she told the young cops that Brent should have been back by then, they'd probably drive out to the compound themselves to check on him. But if a seasoned detective like Peters had been surprised out there and captured or worse, the two babes in the woods standing before her would be cannon fodder.

"Mrs. Bee?"

She shook her head. "I need to speak with Detective Nightshade." He'd worked undercover when Parks was still running his cult. Nightshade probably knew the place better than Flo did. Or at least as well.

"I doubt he'll be in again today," the curly headed cop said on a grin. "I heard he was puking his guts out."

Manchion sipped his coffee before shaking his head. "Nightshade's got that flu that's going around. I hear it's really bad." He narrowed his gaze on Flo. Unlike his partner, he seemed to register her desperation. "Tell us what's wrong and we'll try to help."

Flo thought about it for a beat and then decided it was the best she could do. "Detective Peters went out to the old cult compound looking for my friend, Trisha Colombo. He left hours ago and should have been back by now. I'm worried about them."

The two cops exchanged a look. They set their coffee mugs down and fixed her with a look. "Tell us where he went."

Flo did, and then watched as they checked their duty belts and left, assuring her they'd find her friends.

More cops started to file into the room and Flo stood there, feeling as if she'd jump right out of her skin if she didn't move.

She grabbed her purse and headed for the door. She was tired of waiting and decided that taking action couldn't hurt any more than sitting around had.

Her friends were eating breakfast when she returned to Silver Hills.

Roger jumped up when he spotted her, his handsome face filled with concern. "There you are, doll. I've been looking all over for you. I called several times."

Flo realized she hadn't looked at her cell for hours. "My phone's probably dead. I'm sorry, Roger." Something in her voice must have warned him. He dropped an arm around her shoulders. "Tell me. Whatever it is we'll fix it together."

She sighed, her gaze sliding to Agnes. Her friend took one look at Flo and grabbed a biscuit, pushing away from the table. "It's not that simple, Roger."

Agnes hurried over. "TC?"

Flo nodded. "Parks has her at the complex."

Agnes frowned. "Let's go then."

Flo nodded. It took her a moment to realize Roger was coming along. He reached the door ahead of them, his long strides eating up the lobby faster than theirs. She looked up at him as she passed by and slipped outside. "You're not going to try to talk me out of it?"

Roger's expression was pained but filled with resolution. "I'd love to. But I know you won't listen anyway so I thought I'd save us both the time and trouble and just come along. At least that way I can try to keep you safe."

Tears burned in Flo's gaze. "It might be dangerous."

He lifted an eyebrow, pointing to a big, old Cadillac parked in the front row. "We'll take my car." He opened the passenger side door for Flo as Agnes slipped into the backseat. As he walked around the car, Flo turned and filled her friend in. "Detective Peters left at one AM to get her and he hasn't come back."

Agnes shook her head. "Parks probably got him. He never believed the man was dangerous."

Flo nodded. "I know. I'm really worried about that."

Roger climbed behind the wheel and started the car. "Where are we going?"

Flo gave him directions to the campus.

"Strap in, ladies. We're going into hyper-drive."

Despite her worry, Flo couldn't help smiling. She reached over and gave his arm a squeeze. "Thanks for coming, hun."

He grasped her hand, lifting it to his lips and kissing her palm. "There's no place I'd rather be, doll."

They rode in silence for several moments, the car filled with tension.

"I need to get one of these," Agnes said from the back seat as they neared the compound.

Flo turned to find her friend playing with TC's cell phone. "What are you doing with that?"

"I remembered I took a bunch of pictures the other day and I wanted to go through them in case I caught Parks in the hallway or something without realizing it."

"Good idea. Have you found anything?"

"Not Parks. But here's a face I didn't expect to see..." She held the phone out to Flo.

"The gates are closed."

Flo turned back around in her seat and frowned. Sure enough, the big metal gates that had kept unwelcome visitors out of Park's *Kindredship* cult were closed and probably locked. Roger stopped the big car and looked at Flo. "Do you know how to open them?"

Flo shook her head.

Agnes' head appeared between them as she leaned forward. "We can blast through," she suggested.

"I'm game if you are," Roger said.

But Flo knew how much Roger's car meant to him. "Hopefully that won't be necessary." She frowned at the gate.

"What is it, doll?"

"I was just wondering how the two uniformed police got inside with the gate closed."

"Maybe they closed it behind them."

Flo nodded, "Maybe."

Agnes slid across the seat. "I'll go see if it's unlocked. Maybe we'll get lucky."

Of course, they couldn't be that lucky.

Flo called Agnes back to the car several minutes later, after her friend had determined that the gate was chained with a padlock. She'd tried to squeeze through but only managed to nearly get stuck between the halves of the big gate. Then she'd tried to climb over it, but barely made it a foot before falling back to the ground. Desperation ate at Flo, making her stomach churn. "There has to be a way inside." Then she remembered something from the last time they'd needed to breech the campus's protections. Something Jamie's pops had told them. She turned to Roger. "I think I remember hearing that the river is really low right now."

He nodded. "It hasn't rained in over a month. Why?"

It was a long shot, but Flo couldn't think of anything better at the moment. "Do you know how to get to the river from here?"

"There's a turn-off up the road about a quarter mile."

Agnes slipped back into the car. "We're going to have to blast through," she told them.

Flo shook her head. "Hopefully not." She looked across the car. "Roger?"

"Your wish is my command, doll."

THE "ROAD" WAS REALLY more of a narrow break in the trees. The hard mud that formed the passage was rutted and obscured by over-reaching vegetation on both sides. The big Caddy bounced and swerved along the passage, branches scraping across the windshield and the sides with alarming regularity. Flo skimmed Roger a look and found his face taut, big hands white knuckled on the steering wheel. "You doing okay, hun?"

He nodded. "I think I lost a kidney back there."

She chuckled. "We should be close."

"Stop!" Agnes sat forward, pointing to a spot in the trees where the road took a quick turn.

Flo didn't see the demolished cruiser at first. The sun was shining into the trees, creating a dappled effect that concealed the crash site from view. But she did finally see it, her pressure spiking with alarm at the sight.

As soon as Roger braked to a stop, she and Agnes climbed out of the car. Behind them, Roger called her name as she ran toward the crashed cruiser. The curly haired cop was behind the wheel, his head resting on a deflated airbag and blood oozing down his face from a long cut on his temple. Footsteps hurried up behind them and Flo turned as Roger gently set her aside. "Let me see."

Roger placed two long fingers on the cop's throat and turned to Flo. "His pulse is strong. It looks like he was just knocked out."

"Thank goodness. We should call for an ambulance."

Roger nodded.

Flo peered past the young cop, frowning. "There should be another uniformed officer."

"We need to find him fast." Agnes was staring at the front of the cruiser, frowning.

Flo hurried around to her friend. "Why? What do you see?" But Agnes didn't need to tell her. Three round holes decorated the windshield of the cruiser, the glass fracturing outward from each tidy circle. "Oh my!"

Roger shook his head. "We need to get some help here."

"I agree," Flo said. She noted the surprise in his blue gaze. "You call for help and stay with this young man. Agnes and I will search the immediate area and see if we can find the other uniformed officer."

Roger was already shaking his head before she finished. "Not a chance, doll. It's too dangerous. You don't know if the person who fired these shots is still out there."

"No," she responded. "I don't. But I do know there's a young cop who's injured and needs our help." She pointed to a trail of blood in the dirt. "And beyond that, TC and Detective Peters are in danger. I sat around waiting for someone else to fix this all night. Don't ask me to do it again, Roger. I won't take it well."

He stared at her for a long moment and then expelled air in a frustrated rush of breath. "Okay. You win. But I'm coming with you. We'll call for an ambulance and then try to find the wounded police officer together."

She gave him a brisk nod, relief flooding her. If he'd insisted on her staying behind, Flo would have gotten angry and then he would have gotten angry and then she would have done what she wanted anyway. Flo was much happier having Roger on her side rather than against her.

Even if he was more accustomed to litigating criminals in a courtroom, than going up against them physically.

CHAPTER SEVENTEEN

THE HEAT WAS CLIMBING as they fought their way through the jungle-like vegetation. The poor imitation of a road had ended not too much past where the cruiser had come to its ungainly rest in the trees and they were reduced to following a narrow path while searching for drops of blood that grew scarcer as they walked. "I don't like the looks of this," Agnes said for about the tenth time. "He's gotten a lot clumsier, like he's getting weak." She pointed to a badly broken plant alongside the path. It was mashed in the center as if he'd fallen to the ground there and blood drops speckled the dirt and leaves.

"You're very good at this tracking thing, Agnes," Roger mused aloud.

"Girl scouts," she responded with a proud grin. "I had a lot of wilderness badges."

"That's good," Flo said, grimacing as she slapped a bug away from her sweaty face. "Because this is about as close to wilderness as we're going to get in central Indiana."

Roger moved along carefully in front of them, a long, thick branch in his hand, which he used to clear vegetation and as a walking stick over the rougher areas of the pathway. "I hear the river up ahead."

They all stopped and listened. Sure enough, the angry roar of moving water filled the air.

"That sounds like it's moving pretty fast for not having had any rain lately," Flo said on a frown.

"It's kind of a rapids area," Roger told her, peering in that direction. "I remember this section of the river from a canoe trip I took with friends. The river drops a bit downstream but before it does, there's a wide section where there are some really big boulders. The water hits those rocks pretty fast on the way to the drop."

Flo didn't like the sound of that. If they were going to have to navigate the river she wanted it to be gentle and slow moving. She didn't even know if Agnes could swim. "Let's hope it's low enough that we don't need to get near the water."

"What exactly do you have in mind, doll?"

Flo shook her head. "I'll know better once we see what we're dealing with."

"Shhhh!"

Flo stopped as Agnes' hand found her arm. "What's wrong?"

"I hear something moving up ahead."

Sure enough, there was a soft swish of vegetation on the path ahead and, if they listened really carefully, some heavy breathing too. Roger motioned toward the plants at the side of the path and lifted the stick, ready to pummel someone with it if he needed to. Flo and Agnes eyed the wet, probably critter ridden vegetation and shared a frown. The message sliding silently between them was, "Uh, uh. No way am I crouching in there. I'd rather face off with a murderer."

The leaves up ahead trembled and Flo and Agnes braced themselves in case they needed to run. Roger spread his hands wider on the stick, no doubt thinking he could control it better that way.

A face suddenly appeared above the plants and the newcomer stopped, blinking rapidly. His pale face flushed slightly when he realized who they were. "You scared the stuffing out of me." He frowned. "Mrs. Bee, what are you doing out here?"

Flo hurried over to the young cop as Roger lowered his stick. "Apparently, we're saving you, hun." She reached a hand helplessly toward his shoulder, which was bleeding profusely and looked painful. "Have you been shot?"

The young cop shook his head. "I was jabbed by a tree limb when we crashed. But it hurts like the dickens."

"I'll bet." Flo glanced past him. "Did you see who shot at you?"

The young man frowned. "Unfortunately, not. We never saw it coming. We were bumping along and then all of the sudden the windshield exploded and we were barreling toward the trees. I realized after we crashed that someone was shooting at us." He frowned. "Is officer Blunt okay?"

Flo nodded. "He seems to be."

"We called for an ambulance," Roger told the cop.

"Good."

"Why were you walking out here?" Agnes asked him. "The shooter could still be in the woods."

Flo and Roger shared a small smile as Agnes basically used his argument against the cop. "I was talking on my phone to my girlfriend when we crashed. It flew out of the car and was totaled. The radio doesn't work and Mike's phone is dead. I thought if I could get to the compound I could maybe find a land line or something." He shrugged. "It was a dumb idea. I'd have been better off heading back to the road and trying to flag down a passing car."

"You know a way into the complex?"

"There's a tunnel. That's where we were heading when we couldn't get through the gates."

"You don't have bolt cutters in your squad car, son?" Roger lifted a censoring eyebrow and the kid flushed.

"We did. But I borrowed them last week and forgot to put them back."

Roger shook his head, clearly lamenting the folly of youth.

"Why didn't you use the tunnel?" Agnes asked.

"Oh, I did. But when I got inside and saw how far away the buildings were, I decided it would be better to try the road."

Roger shook his head. "The road's probably just as far, son."

"I know. I guess I'm a little scattered from the crash." Manchion scrubbed a hand over his clammy brow. "I'm not thinking straight."

Flo stepped around him and started down the path, Roger calling her name as she moved more deeply into the woods. Agnes soon pounded heavily up behind her. "I'm having really mixed feelings about this, Flo."

"Yeah, me too, hun. Let's just hope this time things don't go as badly as they did the last time we were here."

Roger and the young cop joined them as they stepped out of the woods and found themselves facing the river. Flo flicked them a quick glance and saw that Roger was wearing just his undershirt. Manchion had something that looked suspiciously like Roger's shirt tied around his neck like a sling.

The cop gave her a quelling look. "Mrs. Bee, you need to stay away from this mess."

She shook her head. "Not going to happen, Officer Manchion. You might as well just suck that down and tell us how we can find my friends."

He gave her a hard look for a moment and then shook his head.

"I told ya, son," Roger said. "The woman has many fine qualities. But she's as stubborn as they come."

Manchion sighed. "Okay, you all stay behind me then. I have the gun."

"You said yourself that you're not thinking clearly," Flo argued. "I'm not sure that's such a good idea."

"We got him some pain meds and water," Roger assured her. "I have a kit in my car. He'll be okay now that he's hydrated. Better than we are anyway. At least he's had some training."

Flo wasn't stupid. She was okay with letting the professionals protect them. As long as they didn't ask her to stay in the background when it came to saving TC. "Fine. Where's this tunnel you used?"

Manchion jerked his head toward a copse of evergreens. "Under here. As you can see, it's well hidden. It looks like the cultists thought they needed a back way out of the complex."

"Of course, they did," Flo murmured.

Manchion grabbed a large branch covered in soft pine needles and ducked under it, quickly disappearing from sight.

Roger held the same branch back for Flo and Agnes and then ducked in behind them. It was cooler under the massive evergreen trees, and smelled nice, fragrant with the scent of mashed pine needles. The fence on the side of the property that bordered the hidden road was old, built of cracked and mis-shapen stone that had been shored up with lots of mortar. But the section under the trees looked newer and it was built of red brick instead of stone. Flo didn't see Manchion or the tunnel at first. All she saw were trees. But then a branch quivered and the young cop stuck his head through. "Looks clear. Come on."

The tunnel was short, really only about five feet long, and emptied out into the very back of the enormous complex. Flo squinted at the buildings in the distance, recognizing the annex where young Jamie had been held prisoner the last time they were there and the main building high on the hill a distance away.

From where they stood they couldn't even see the front gates.

Manchion took a deep breath. "Come on, folks. We've got quite a walk ahead of us."

As they neared the annex, Flo turned away from the path. "This way, Officer Manchion. There should be golf carts in this building. It'll be easier to cover the rest of the distance on them."

The cop frowned, shaking his head. "It's going to be hard to sneak up on somebody in a golf cart."

"He's right, doll. Driving up to the front door isn't exactly a stealthy move."

She grinned. "Exactly. Parks won't expect Agnes and I to be stealthy. He also won't be worried about us. But while we're distracting him, you two can circle around and catch him by surprise."

"Ahh," Roger said with an approving glance. "Smart."

"Thanks."

Flo looked at Manchion. He didn't look as convinced. "What if he shoots first and asks questions later?"

She tried not to think about that possibility. It was a remote one. But she had to admit there was a small chance Parks would attack them. "He's not exactly afraid of us, Officer. That's going to be his Achilles heel."

Manchion moved his arm and winced as his wound no doubt screamed from the action. Finally, he sighed. "Okay. I don't see that we have a lot of choices here. I'm not really in any shape to go hand to hand with the man. But I want to go on record as not liking this one bit."

"Noted." Flo looked at Agnes. "Let's go grab a golf cart. Hopefully there's still one with some juice in it."

Roger and Manchion fell in behind them as they approached the annex. Flo noted that the young cop had his gun in his hand and a wary look in his eyes. Manchion was spooked and she didn't blame him one bit. As Cook would say, being a voodoo practitioner from Louisiana, the compound had seriously bad juju. It also had to be a bit surreal to the young cop to be going into a potentially dangerous situation wounded, and with three senior citizens as his backup instead of his partner.

Fortunately for Manchion, Flo and Agnes had two things going for them that he didn't have. 1. Previous experience with both Parks and his compound, and 2. A determination to save TC and Peters that superseded even common sense.

Okay. Maybe that last thing wasn't a positive. But unfortunately, it was a reality.

Flo pointed to the garage-sized door at one end of the annex and Agnes nodded. Her friend tip-toed theatrically up to the long, narrow window and peered inside. After a moment she nodded and turned to Manchion. Agnes lifted two fingers into a "vee" and pointed to her own eyes with them, then pointed them at Manchion and jerked her head toward the main building.

He frowned. "What's that supposed to mean?"

Agnes looked surprised. "I thought you'd know. Hand signals are on all the cop shows."

Manchion rolled his eyes. "Not *those* hand signals. And I'm not leaving until I see you safely on a cart."

Though Agnes looked disgusted by his lack of common cop sign language, she reached down and tried to pull the door open. It wouldn't budge. "Let's see if there's a side door," Flo suggested. "I'm sure there's a door opener inside."

Agnes drifted around one side and Flo the other. Manchion stood in front, his head on a swivel looking for movement around them. The door Flo was looking for was near the back of the building on the annex side. Flo headed for it, cognizant only of the need to hurry. She reached for the door just as Roger called her name and turned the knob before looking in his direction. "I'll open the big door from inside. Wait for me there."

Roger shook his head frowning. He picked up the pace and Flo pushed the door open. It was pitch black in the building. Even the narrow windows at the front didn't offer much light. She took a couple of steps inside and ran her hand along the wall, looking for a switch.

The only warning she got that she was not alone was the soft scuff of a shoe just behind her. Flo didn't even have time to turn her head before some kind of coarse fabric was tugged over her head and she was jerked roughly backward. She gave a surprised yelp and kicked out but she was quickly subdued. "Roger!" she screamed, the sound muffled when the fabric over her head was sucked into her mouth, nearly choking her. Her faint hope that Roger would reach her in time was sliced brutally off at the sound of the lock being shot home on the door. And then she was lifted off her feet, wriggling and kicking, and dropped into an opening that smelled like dead worms and rot.

CHAPTER EIGHTEEN

FLO LANDED HARD AND fell to one hand, the smell of musty dirt rising up to fill her nostrils. She shoved quickly off the ground, knowing her only hope was to catch her attacker by surprise. Hard hands grabbed her shoulders and yanked her upright. Instinctively falling back on the self-defense training she'd taken at the Silver Hills PD, Flo let her knees soften and tumbled downward again, kicking out with her foot in an attempt to trip her attacker up. She connected with a hard limb and earned herself a muttered curse and a smack to the head in return.

Pain flared through her skull and Flo bit her tongue, swallowing the metallic taste of her own blood. The ungentle hands yanked her arms around behind her back. Flo yelled in pain as they wrenched her shoulder. "If you'd behave this wouldn't be necessary," a gruff, angry voice growled. Something that felt thin enough to cut the skin snaked around her wrists and tightened painfully.

She figured they were zip ties.

Flo struggled to remember what she'd learned in her class about getting free from zip ties, but she was having trouble forming a coherent thought after the blow to her head.

The attacker grabbed her arms and yanked her roughly to her feet and then shoved her forward. "No more funny business or your friends are gonna pay for it."

The voice was forceful and gruff. It sounded like the voice of someone who'd smoked a lot of cigarettes over the years. But there was an undertone to it that seemed familiar. If only she could put a name to it.

Was it Parks?

Possibly.

But she just couldn't be sure. She'd have to find a way to draw him out into regular conversation. Because it was becoming clear to her that the speaker was disguising his voice.

Which meant it was probably someone she knew.

They walked for a long time through what Flo was beginning to realize was a tunnel of some kind. The occasional glow of light beyond the dense material covering her head told her there were lights at intermittent spots along the way. The ground beneath her feet started out soft but eventually grew moist. Flo figured they had to be in near proximity to either the river or the small pond by the main building. Then it turned hard, almost rocky. Her calves ached so she thought they might be climbing.

The main building was at the top of a hill. Could they be going there?

The temperature never varied. It was cold the entire time they walked the passage. Bone-chillingly cold. And Flo realized they had to be deep underground.

The thought made her heart race with fear. She'd always been terrified by the idea of being buried alive.

What if that was what her abductor had in mind? Was he going to abandon her in the underground tunnel and walk away, leaving her bound and blinded to die? How long had it been since she'd felt the man's hands on her back, shoving her forward? Or heard his hated voice?

She couldn't remember and panic rose to make it hard to breathe. "What are you going to do to me?"

No response.

Flo jerked to a stop and tried to turn. "Where am I?" She was shocked by the terror throbbing in her voice.

"Just keep going or I'll *make* you move."

Relief flooded. Flo took a deep breath and started to move. But she crashed into a lumpy, flannel covered chest and soon found herself on her butt in the dirt again when he shoved her.

She'd apparently gotten turned around.

"Flip around and start walking."

Flo fought to get to her feet, finding it all but impossible with her hands behind her back. But she finally managed by rolling over onto her knees and straining her thighs to stand.

"Walk," the hated voice told her.

And, having no other choice, she did.

Flo was so tired she was stumbling by the time he told her to stop. She stood panting, legs shaky with weariness, and so cold her teeth were clacking together hard enough to chip.

He stopped behind her, his breath rasping against her ear as he bent closer. "I'm going to cut you loose and you're going to climb the ladder in front of you. No funny business. You understand?"

She frowned, something inside of her wanting so badly to resist, but she finally gave him a tight nod. His threat about hurting her friends was more than she could ignore.

When her hands were free she slowly pulled her arms forward, groaning with pain.

"Climb!"

Flo took a step forward, testing the air blindly with her hands until she encountered the unmistakable shape and hardness of metal rungs. Then she felt her way onto the first one and began to climb, moving slowly because she was so disoriented from not being able to see her surroundings. Eventually her head rose into a space that felt entirely different and warmth oozed into her aching muscles from above. She felt a wood floor beneath her hands and eased herself over the lip of the opening until her legs were free of the hole. She expected the man to climb out after her but instead she heard the hatch she'd climbed through slam closed and the sound of a latch snapping home.

Flo sat up and yanked off the bag, her bouff snapping with electricity as she pulled it free.

She looked around, finding herself in a room just like the one she'd been held in the previous time she'd been there. A colorful rag rug lay bunched up next to the hatchway and Flo couldn't help wondering if there'd been a hatch in the previous room too.

At first, she thought she was alone. But then she spied the long, slender shape under a blanket in the room's only bed and she jumped to her feet with a cry. Long, dark hair spilled over the pillow and a blanket was pulled up to nearly cover the face beneath the hair.

"TC!" Flo hurried around the bed, bending to push the thick curtain of silky hair from her friend's attractive face. TC's cheeks were flushed, her skin warm and she seemed to be breathing evenly. Flo sagged to the bed with relief.

She was alive.

But she was sleeping much too deeply. Flo realized in that moment that TC had been drugged. Unconscious, she would prove no challenge to the kidnapper. But that meant she was completely helpless. Flo needed to get her friend out of there and fast.

She slapped TC gently on the cheek. "TC, wake up, hun. I came to help but I can't do it alone." TC didn't respond. There wasn't even a fluttering of her lashes to tell Flo she was aware of her presence. Flo slapped her again, a little harder. "TC! Come on, hun. You have to shake this off."

She looked around and saw a pitcher of water on the dresser. Déjà vu hit her hard. Flo's heart beat against her ribs, panic flaring at the memory of that previous time, spent in a room much like the one she was currently standing in.

She shook it off. She had something she needed to do and she couldn't afford to fall apart.

Not yet.

Flo hurried over and poured some of the water into a glass. That was when her gaze lifted to the painting above the dresser and she remembered.

The camera!

Flo spotted the small, blinking light and rage flared. "I don't think so!" She threw the glass of water at the painting, drenching the tiny light and the painting around it. Unhappily, the blinking didn't stop. Flo would give anything for a stick of gum like she'd used to cover the tiny camera the previous time.

But since she didn't have any, she would need to try something a bit more drastic.

She'd have to take the painting down so she could get to the camera. Flo grasped the frame and tugged. It didn't move. Evidently, it was anchored to the wall. She shoved hard on the wood and managed to crack it in the top corner. Another hard shove splintered the frame on the bottom corner and Flo wrenched it away from the wall. Then she used the piece of wood to pry the painting loose. It broke away in pieces but she soon exposed the camera, which had been mounted in a spot where a large rose in the painting had hidden it from sight. Flo yanked a large metal tack from the broken wood and gouged the drywall around the camera until she exposed one of the wires. Then she tugged on the wire until it came loose.

Finally, the little blinking light stopped blinking.

"Jerks!" Flo muttered. She swiped a hand over her brow, surprised to find it moist. The room was unusually hot. Of course, with the compound being deserted the power had probably been shut off.

Flo refilled the glass with water. Behind her the bed creaked and Flo whipped around, hopeful that TC was finally waking up.

Her friend's eyes were still closed.

She hurried over to the bed and grabbed the corner of the blanket, tucking it into the water and using it to bathe TC's face and the back of her neck. "Wake up, hun. Brent and I need your help."

TC's eyelids fluttered. She made a small sound and licked her dry lips. "Brent?"

"That's right, hun. You've been drugged. You need to fight your way out of it."

TC gave her head a little shake and seemed to be settling back to sleep.

Flo grimaced. "I really didn't want to do this to you but..." She dumped the glass of water over TC's head.

Her friend's eyes shot open and she swung a defensive fist in Flo's direction as she gave a soft squeal of alarm.

Flo jumped out of reach. "Sorry, hun. I had to wake you up."

TC scraped water from her face and shoved wet hair off her throat where it clung. "My head's killing me."

Flo wrapped an arm around TC's shoulders. "Sit up slowly. I'm sure you're dehydrated and you probably haven't eaten for a while. The drugs have hit you pretty hard." She went back to the pitcher and refilled the glass, supporting TC while she drank it down. "That's better. Now lean against these pillows while I tell you what's going on."

Over the next several minutes, TC slowly eased out of the last vestiges of the drug. She seemed weary as Flo told her the story, but she gained energy and interest when Flo got to the part where Brent had come to save her. "Have you seen him?"

TC shook her head. She scrubbed a shaky hand over her mouth, her eyes dark pools of concern. "Flo, what if he was hurt? Or worse?"

Flo bit the inside of her lip. All she could think about was the crashed cruiser and the bloodless, pain-filled faces of the two young detectives. "I'm sure he's holding his own, wherever he is, hun. But if we're going to help him we need to get out of here."

TC nodded and tried to swing her legs over the edge of the bed.

Flo stopped her. "Just give yourself a few more minutes to kick off this drug. I need to ask you some questions."

TC leaned her head back with a sigh. "Okay."

"Did you see who abducted you?"

"No. I was leaving Silver Hills last night..." She frowned. "Was it last night?" She gave her head a little shake. "Whenever it was. I'd just unlocked my car door and was opening it when something stung my neck. I have a distant memory of voices and of being shoved into my car and then nothing."

"You don't remember being propped in a chair and having a picture taken?"

"No." Her green gaze went wide. "They sent you a picture of me?"

"It was terrifying. You had one of those over your head..." Flo pointed to the bag she'd flung across the room when she ripped it off. "But I could still tell it was you. You were tied to the arms and legs of the chair and your head was drooping like you were..." Flo swallowed hard.

TC reached out and squeezed her hand. "I'm fine, Flo. Really."

Flo nodded, pulling a shaky breath into her lungs. "There's been no ransom call. No explanation for why you were taken..."

"Why do *you* think I'm here?"

Flo thought about it for a moment and then went with the easiest explanation. "They didn't bother to hide your location in the picture. They knew I'd recognize this room and come for you. It's the only thing I can think of."

"Then it's someone who knew you were held here?"

"Yes. I believe it's Buddy Parks."

TC shook her head. "I'm sorry. I can't tell you it was him for sure. But even if it was, he wasn't working alone. I'm almost certain there was someone else with him."

Flo thought about this for a moment and then nodded. "Okay, hun. We'll figure it out. First things first. Are you feeling strong enough to try to get out of here?"

There was a muffled sound near the door and Flo held up a hand to silence TC. They waited for a moment but the door didn't open. Flo moved closer. She pressed an ear against the wood, hearing nothing. Then she got down on her knees and tried to look under the door. She couldn't see anything. It was as if it was blocked.

"What's happening?" TC asked from just behind Flo.

Flo looked up at her friend, a feeling of impending doom making her chest tight. "I don't know..."

A slightly sweet, metallic scent filled her nostrils and she looked up at the soft whisper of sound coming from the vent high on the wall. That wasn't right. If the power was off...

TC's gaze followed hers. "What is that?"

"Flo pushed to her feet. "I don't know, but whatever it is, I'm sure it's not good. We need to get out of here, fast.

TC giggled.

Flo threw her a look of outrage. "This isn't funny, T..." TC's eyes widened, the whites huge. She lifted her face to the vent and sucked in a big breath. "I like."

Flo sagged against the door, trying to remember what she'd been worried about. It was important. She remembered that. But she couldn't for the life of her remember why.

TC started to dance around the room. She shook her booty and then dissolved into laughter as she bumped up against the dresser and knocked the pitcher off onto the floor. Flo laughed too. "You're a terrible dancer."

TC hurried over and grabbed Flo's hand, yanking her away from the wall and bowing low as she chuckled. "Will you do me the honors?"

Flo would have, but she was suddenly light-headed and her stomach was starting to burn. "I don't think..." she turned away and retched.

"Ew!," TC said. "Gross."

Flo threw up violently, feeling as if her stomach was trying to escape through her esophagus, and then stood there, gasping. "TC, snap out of it. That's some kind of gas and if we don't..." She retched again.

A moment later TC fell backward on the bed, her eyes rolling closed.

"TC!" Flo stumbled over to her friend and grabbed her hand. It was like ice. "Hun, you need to wake up."

TC's pretty face split in a smile. "I'm awake."

Flo sagged downward. "Oh, thank the Lord." Weariness swamped her, turning her muscles to noodles. Flo wobbled. Her lids grew heavy.

Suddenly the bed jumped up and smacked her on the back of the head. A small part of Flo's brain knew they couldn't stay where they were. But she couldn't move even to save her own life. TC groaned. That was when Flo realized she had to find a way to kick off the effects or her friend was going to die too. And TC had her whole life ahead of her.

Flo slid her fingers across the covers until she found TC's hand. Concentrating as hard as her fuzzy brain would allow, Flo forced her fingertips together and pinched TC's hand. TC twitched but didn't rouse. Flo tried again, gritting her teeth to pinch harder the second time.

"Ow..." TC murmured.

"Get up..." Flo licked impossibly dry lips, concentrating on pinching her friend again.

TC pushed Flo's hand away. "Okay, mom. I'm getting up."

"Give me a hand..." Flo told her, lifting her arm as TC rolled unsteadily to her feet. TC blinked several times, clearly confused, and then frowned down at Flo. "You're not my mom."

"Lord help me," Flo muttered.

Just then a terrifying sound ate through the weakness in her limbs and Flo suddenly found the energy to push slowly to her elbows. It was the sound of a bolt sliding back. Flo's gaze skimmed to the hatch in the floor, her pulse spiking. The rush of adrenaline dispelled some of the effects of the drug and Flo suddenly knew. "They're coming back!"

Regrettably, she knew one other thing. Whatever their captors had planned, Flo and TC would be all but helpless to stop them.

CHAPTER NINETEEN

FLO GRABBED TC'S ARM and leaned close to whisper. "Grab a piece of that glass."

As TC staggered across the room to comply, Flo looked around for something else she could use as a weapon. There wasn't much. But her gaze fell on the piece of frame she'd pried loose from the wall and she grabbed it. "Hurry!" She moved as quickly as she could across the room, stumbling once as the drug in the air made her dizzy again. She stood to one side of the hatch and lifted her board. TC stood on the other side, a long, deadly looking sliver of glass clutched in her hand like a dagger. TC's lids looked painfully heavy and she wavered on her feet. Flo prayed she'd be able to use the glass she clutched in her hand.

The hatch eased open a fraction of an inch and stopped. Flo held her breath, her hands tightening on the board. The silence throbbed with menace and Flo's chest started to hurt. When the hatch didn't open any farther, she worried the person on the ladder had spotted them and she eased quietly back, toward the hinge side of the opening.

The hatch opened another half an inch and stopped again while Flo forced herself to breathe. Suddenly the hatch flew backward, smacking into the floor behind it and barely missing Flo's leg as it flew past. A gun came through the hole, clutched in a pale hand, and Flo swung the board. The man holding the gun just had time to turn, eyes wide with surprise, as Flo slammed the frame down on his head.

He cried out and dropped the gun as TC lunged.

Just as her friend swung her hand downward, Flo realized their mistake. "No, TC!"

Fortunately, officer Manchion's training kicked in and he dodged out of the way as the deadly sliver sliced through the air where his shoulder had been. He reached up and wrapped strong fingers around TC's wrist, tugging her off balance as she cried out in rage.

Flo hurried around the opening, wrapping her arms around TC to keep her from throwing herself at the young cop. "TC, stop! This is Officer Manchion. He's with us."

TC dropped to her knees, her chest heaving, and scraped a hand over her moist face. "I don't feel so good."

Flo looked at the cop. "They're pumping some kind of gas into this room."

He nodded, his nostrils flaring. "Smells like nitrous oxide. If this room is airtight it could be deadly."

Flo's gaze slid to the blocked opening beneath the room's only door. "Help me get her on the ladder."

Between them, they managed to ease TC down the ladder. At the bottom, Manchion passed her off to Roger and climbed back up to make sure Flo didn't miss a step in her drugged state.

Agnes hurried over and grabbed Flo under the arms as her foot hit the dirt.

"I can't believe you found us," she told her friend.

Agnes gave her a rare hug. "I was so worried."

"Are you okay, doll? You look pretty shaky." Roger's handsome face was filled with fear.

Flo figured if he weren't all but holding TC on her feet, he'd be glued to her side, fussing. "I'm fine, hun. Just a little groggy from whatever they were pumping into that room."

Manchion closed the hatch and locked it again. "We need to get topside ASAP. We spotted Detective Peters' car behind that annex."

TC's eyes went wide. "He *did* come." She grabbed Flo's arm in a desperate grip. "We need to help him, Flo."

"We will, hun. Don't worry."

Manchion started off, his gun still clutched in his hand.

Flo looked wearily down the long passageway. She'd known it felt endless when she was being forced to walk blindly along its length, but seeing it was disheartening. It looked like it went on forever. She hurried her steps to catch up with Manchion. Lowering her voice, she spoke softly enough that the others couldn't hear. "It's a really long walk back, Officer."

He nodded. "Fortunately, there's an offshoot not too far up that I'm guessing leads to the main building."

Flo frowned. "I'll bet it goes to the office."

He looked at her.

"The woman who ran the cult was big on keeping her role a secret. I'll bet she used these tunnels to move around undetected."

"I hope you're right, Mrs. Bee. Because if there *is* an office, whoever's running this operation now will no doubt be using it."

Flo nodded, dropping back to help Roger with TC, who was still pretty unsteady. He shook his head. "I'm surprised she's still so out of it. She's young and healthy."

"She'd already been drugged when I found her. Her system's probably reeling under this new stuff."

"Did I hear Officer Manchion say it was nitrous oxide?"

"He did."

"Laughing gas," Agnes said with a shake of her head. "Apparently it's no laughing matter."

"Here's our turn-off," Manchion told them. He pointed to a passageway that fed off the main one. The offshoot was considerably narrower than the passage, barely wider than the men's shoulders. It didn't look all that long but Flo thought it narrowed even further by the time it ended. She felt panic rising at the idea of going in. Her face broke out in clammy sweat.

"You look a little green. Are you going to get sick?" Roger asked.

Flo shook her head, one hand holding her churning stomach. "Let's just get this over with."

There was a distant clunking sound and, one by one all down the passageway, all the lights blinked out, leaving them in total, unrelenting darkness.

They stood in shocked silence for a moment and then an unhappy voice said. "Well poop."

Flo couldn't agree with Agnes more. "Are you all still here?"

She felt a warm hand on her arm and Roger gave her a squeeze. "Right here, doll."

TC coughed wetly on Roger's other side, sounding as if she was going to be sick.

"Watch your shoes, Roger." Flo could almost feel his confusion.

"What?"

TC gagged violently and then let fly. Roger yelped and danced sideways. "Dangit!"

"Sorry, Roger." TC sounded so miserable, Flo knew Roger would forgive her for horking on his shoes.

"It's okay, dear."

Flo felt a presence coming up behind her and yelped as a big hand clamped onto her shoulder. A light flicked on, illuminating a wide, distorted face. Flo yelped again and Agnes glowered. "You don't look so hot either."

"Sorry, hun. You surprised me."

She held up TC's cell phone. "This thing isn't good for much down here but it does have a handy dandy light on it."

Manchion's tall form hovered on the edge of the light. "Lead on, Miss Willard."

Agnes did as he asked, moving in front of the group to illuminate the shorter passage. Flo had thought it looked narrow from outside looking in, but once she was inside she realized just how bad it was. The thing was barely wider than her own shoulders, let alone those of the men and Agnes. Her friend shuffled forward carefully, jumping occasionally when her arms touched the rough sides. By the time they reached the end, Flo was pretty sure they were all as frantic as she was to climb out of it.

That was when she thought of something that made her heart pound so hard she felt dizzy. What if it was a trap? The passage wasn't really wide enough for people to pass through. They'd only taken it out of a sense of urgency and more than a little desperation. Agnes skimmed the dull light of the phone around the walls and ceiling and Flo's panic rose. She didn't see any openings.

She turned as Roger and TC reached her, their tall bodies squished into a space that Flo realized was shorter as well as narrower than when they'd begun. "We need to get out of here!"

Roger frowned. "Take a breath, doll. It's going to be okay."

"Um..." Agnes' voice was louder than it should have been. Agnes tended to get loud when she was nervous. "Is this light..."

The already dull light flickered and went out. For the second time in minutes they were plunged into impenetrable darkness. But they were squished into a much smaller space...elbow to elbow and knee to knee. Flo clenched her hands and took several deep breaths trying to calm down. It was all she could do to keep from shoving Roger out of the way and running screaming from the place. She'd always been a little claustrophobic, but what she was feeling wasn't a "little" anything. The ribbon of claustrophobia she'd always suspected she had was roaring like a lion through her system, making her skin jump and her stomach clench. "I have to get out of here."

She tried to squeeze past Roger and came up against a dirty rock wall. Chunks of dirt filtered down, landing in her hair and snaking into her mouth. Flo spit dirt and felt her panic rise another notch. She was wedged against the unmoving wall, with Agnes looming on one side and Roger taking up all the available space on the other side. Behind him, unseen but thickening the wall trapping her in that space, was Officer Manchion. The young cop's breaths rasped loudly through the silence and Flo couldn't help wondering if he was feeling what she was.

TC's soft moaning only added to the horror clawing through Flo's chest.

She started to breathe heavily, her hands scrabbling at the rock as, in pure terror, she tried to dig her way out.

"Flo, you need to calm down," Agnes told her. Her friend reached out and grabbed Flo's hand through the darkness, startling her. Flo yelped, yanking her arm from Agnes' grip. The quick, fierce reaction caught Agnes off guard and caused her to fall forward. She hit the wall, her hands slapping against the rock in an effort to keep from falling forward and sending Roger, Flo and TC to the floor like bowling pins. With a drawn-out scraping sound and a muttered, "Umph!" Agnes hit the dirt. Flo knew that because her friend sent a cloud of the silty dust into the air when she landed.

Flo turned away and pushed at the first thing that got in her way. Her heart was pounding so hard she thought she might pass out.

Sudden pain blossomed on Flo's cheek. Her head snapped back and TC's soft voice swam between them.

"I'm sorry, Flo. But you needed that."

Flo closed her eyes, breathing deeply. She knew her friend was right but she was still shocked by the slap.

The world rumbled.

Dirt filtered down on their heads and Flo's panic flared again. "Earthquake!" She screamed and tried to barrel past TC. She didn't get far. There was just no room to move in the passage.

A throaty yell brought Flo whipping around. She was certain she'd find Agnes covered in debris flailing for her life.

Instead, light shimmered into the narrow space.

Agnes was lying face first on an oriental rug, her back half still in the passageway, and a man holding a gun was staring down at her with confusion on his face.

Officer Manchion stepped forward, lifting his weapon. "Drop the gun."

The man standing over Agnes frowned, his slightly bulging brown gaze narrowing in thought. Then he shook his head, his gun lowering toward Agnes. "I think you'd better drop *your* gun."

Flo couldn't believe her eyes. She gaped at the man, thoroughly shocked. "It's not possible!"

Bo Baccarat shrugged. "Why not? I'm as capable as the next guy of using people's gullibility against them."

She tried to peer past him into the room. "I assume your brothers are involved too?"

Bo shrugged. "You know what they say about assuming." He jerked his head toward the gun Manchion was holding. "Put it down."

Flo glanced at Agnes, panic searing through her. Bo had already proved he wasn't afraid to murder people who dared to get in his way. She lifted her hands. "Okay. Just stay calm." She looked at the young cop, whose hand Flo noticed was shaking. "Put your gun down, Officer."

He gave her the side eye, clearly surprised. "That's not going to happen."

"You have to. He'll kill Agnes. I know this man. He's been hiding for years behind social awkwardness but I see now he's a sociopath."

Bo's gaze hardened. "No, Mrs. Bee. I'm a businessman. That's all."

"Killing people is your business?"

He shrugged, a small smile playing across his lips. "Things aren't always what they seem, Mrs. Bee."

"I think more often than not they are, Mr. Baccarat."

"What did you do to Brent?" TC asked, stepping forward. "If you hurt him..."

Bo lifted his brows. "Ah, how sweet. You care about the nosy cop. Don't worry, he's just sleeping over there across the room. For the moment. If he wakes up he's going to have a heck of a headache."

TC's hands fisted at her sides and Flo reached out, grasping one of them and giving it a slight squeeze. "Stay calm, hun. Think of Agnes."

Roger placed a hand on TC's shoulder. "Flo's right. If you go after him you and Agnes won't survive."

"He can only get one of us," TC said in a voice Flo barely recognized.

"And what if it's Agnes?" Flo asked her friend.

TC blinked and then sighed, nodding tightly.

Speaking of Agnes... Flo glanced down, suddenly realizing her friend hadn't moved in moments. Had she hit her head? Agnes' eyes were closed and Flo frowned. She opened her mouth to voice her concern when Agnes' fingers twitched. They twitched again and Flo realized Agnes was trying to tell them something. She skimmed a look toward Manchion and found him frowning. But as she caught his gaze, he gave the slightest nod.

Flo jerked her chin toward Roger.

Manchion lifted his hands. "Okay, I'm putting the gun down."

Bo's gaze stayed locked on the young cop, following the movement of the gun all the way to the ground. Then he motioned with his own weapon. "Okay, inside, all of you."

Agnes twitched her fingers again and Flo clasped TC's hand, squeezing hard. She prayed Manchion got her message about Roger.

"Now!" Agnes yelled and, before Bo could react to her scream, Agnes grabbed his ankles and pulled, rolling sideways to fling him off balance.

Flo tugged TC to the ground while Manchion shoved Roger to the ground and dove for his gun.

Bo started to fall but he pointed his gun at Agnes as he did.

"No!" Flo screamed.

Baccarat's gun went off several times, pinging off the rocky dirt of the passageway, way too near Agnes and TC for Flo's comfort.

Officer Manchion grasped his weapon, rolled onto his belly, and fired.

Bo Baccarat's head snapped back and he went limp, sliding down the side of the opening and landing with his bleeding head on Agnes' pillow-like boohind.

"Are you okay?" Flo yelled as she climbed to her feet and hurried over to her friend.

Agnes groaned and stirred, looking over her shoulder. "I'd be a lot better if this guy wasn't giving me a doggy how-do-ya-do. And he's bleeding all over me."

Flo looked at the young cop. "We'll get him off."

Manchion grabbed Bo's gun and slipped it into the waistband of his uniform slacks. He glanced at his sling and Flo realized he'd have trouble lifting the killer with one arm. "I'll just roll him off."

But it wasn't as easy as rolling him to the side. The opening just wasn't wide enough. Finally, Manchion and Roger each grasped one of Bo's wrists and tugged him into the passage while Agnes scurried to her feet. "Well that was..." The door snapped shut between them and Flo and Co found themselves plunged into darkness for a third time.

Something hit the inside of the door and there was a muffled grunt. Flo ran over and pounded on the wall that served as the opening. "Agnes! Let us in!" She felt Roger moving up next to her.

"There has to be a trigger out here somewhere."

Flo realized he was right. "Everybody over here, run your hands all over this wall here."

A moment later TC called out. "I found it!" There was a small click and the door slid open.

They found themselves staring at Detective Peters, who looked like he'd gone several rounds with a mixed martial arts champion. He had Bill Baccarat on his knees in front of him, hands tied behind his back with some kind of decorative rope, and he was standing over an unconscious Bob with a gun in his hand.

"Brent!" TC shot past Flo and ran to him, flinging herself into his arms.

Flo saw him grimace as his girlfriend barreled into his middle and she realized his injuries didn't stop at his poor, battered face. "Careful, hun. I think Detective Peters is feeling the results of his treatment."

TC jumped away from him like he was on fire. "Oh! I'm so sorry. Are you hurt?"

He was slightly bent, one arm pressed against his side. "Just a few broken ribs. I'll be fine." He scanned Flo a look, giving her a weary smile. "I should have known you wouldn't stay out of this."

Flo returned his smile. "You're welcome."

CHAPTER TWENTY

THEY ALL STARED DOWN at the pictures on TC's phone. Flo shook her head. "I can't believe you had this evidence and didn't tell me."

Agnes bristled. "I tried to show it to you in the car but you got distracted by the locked gate at the compound."

Flo sighed. "You're right."

TC reached for her phone, picking it up and frowning down at the pictures showing the Baccarat brothers talking to Vlad Newsome outside *Nightowl, Inc.* "Do you still think Vlad had something to do with the murders?" TC asked her cop.

Detective Peters shook his head. "Other than the fact that he owns the company, there's nothing at all to tie him to the break-ins or the murders." He glanced at Flo. "Your hunch was right. The brothers were robbing the renters at Mr. Newsome's properties to encourage sales of the new security system."

"But then Parks has to be involved," Flo insisted.

"He might be. But, as usual, we can't pin anything on him."

"I don't understand," said Roger. "Why would the brothers do all this to ensure the sales of something they don't own?"

"They don't own it outright, no," Detective Peters said. "But between them they own a considerable share of company stock. And Bill was Parks' business consultant so he stood to benefit from a successful business model."

Agnes snorted. "That's the first time I've heard murder classified as a successful business model."

Peters shrugged. "Technically, it would be theft. The murder was something else entirely. That was an attempt to stop the Tynes and their fellow litigants from destroying *Nightowl* before *Rest Easy Security* could make their money off the company."

"What's so important about *Nightowl*?" TC asked.

"Nothing really. But Mr. Newsome was their first big client and they saw *Nightowl* as the gateway to all the other big players in rentals."

"You mean the other slumlords," Flo murmured.

"Unfortunately, yes. There's no reason to assume they'd have used any different means to gain customers wherever they set their sights."

"It's diabolical," Roger said, shaking his head

"Yes. It certainly is," Peters agreed.

"But why did they kidnap me?" TC asked, frowning.

Peters reached out and rubbed a hand down her arm, earning himself a smile. "The Baccarats knew Flo's reputation for getting to the bottom of things she'd taken an interest in. When they realized Flo had set her sights on clearing Vlad, they knew it was only a matter of time before she uncovered their part in everything. They used you to lure her out to the compound."

Flo felt a warm bloom in her belly. It was the closest the young detective had ever come to admitting she was doing good work. "Then I guess you'll respect and support our efforts from here on out?"

Peters shook his head. "You nearly got TC killed."

"And you too," TC said, frowning.

Flo tried to capture TC's gaze but her friend refused to look at her. She'd been evading Flo ever since they'd come back from the compound. Agnes was clearly wrong. TC *was* mad at them. And Flo worried she'd never get over it. "I'm really sorry, hun."

TC shrugged.

"It's not our fault," Agnes said, stepping closer to Flo in support. "We were only trying to help Vlad. At Morty's request."

"You didn't trust me to find the truth?" Peters asked. Amazingly, Flo saw hurt in his eyes.

"We do...did. But don't forget you weren't the lead on this at the time. Nightshade was." Flo hoped he didn't mention all the other times when he *was* the lead and she went behind his back to pursue a solution despite his efforts.

Peters just shook his head. To his credit, he wasn't fooled by her objection one little bit.

"It's not that we don't trust you, hun," she said softly. "It's just that I have trouble sitting on my hands if there's something I can do to help." Flo frowned as she remembered how horrible it had been hanging around the police station while Peters went to find TC by himself. And then she remembered how it had turned out. "And we did end up saving you and TC."

Peters flushed, clearly still embarrassed by that. "You did. But I'd still like to put you in jail for obstruction."

"Why haven't you?"

He sighed. "Officer Manchion spoke eloquently on your behalf."

Flo grinned. "He's going to be a great cop."

"Yeah, whatever," Peters said. But there was a flash of humor in his gaze.

Roger glanced at his watch. "We need to get back to Silver Hills, doll. Richard's announcing the two management finalists tonight."

Agnes frowned. "Well, I know one of them won't be me since I never had time to put my application in."

Flo reached out and squeezed her friend's hand. "It's okay, hun. There will be other opportunities."

Agnes didn't look convinced.

Roger and Agnes filed out. Flo told Roger she'd be right behind him. "I need to speak to TC for a moment."

He scanned the younger woman a look and then gave Flo a supportive smile. "We'll wait in the car." Roger caught TC's eye and she flushed, clearly reading something in his gaze.

Peters excused himself too, leaving the two women in the Interview room by themselves.

They stood in uncomfortable silence for a long moment. TC stared down at the table, obviously unwilling to speak first.

Flo decided it was up to her to make the first effort. "I really am sorry, hun."

"I know."

"But you're still mad at me?"

TC shrugged. "Not mad, really. I'm just sick of being speared on the pointy end of your schemes all the time."

"I understand that, Trisha. I really do. If I could change how that thing at *Nightowl* turned out I would. You know that, right?"

TC finally lifted her gaze. "I know you think that, Flo. But when you get your mind around something you just can't let go of it. People around you tend to get hurt and, though you feel bad about it, you don't do anything to change your behavior."

Flo couldn't disagree. "You're right. I've never thought about it that way."

"And that's the nut of the problem. You don't *think* of anything beyond what you've decided you have to do. I'm just not interested in being part of the fallout anymore."

Tears burned Flo's eyes. "I don't want to lose you as a friend, TC."

TC's rigid stance softened. She gave Flo a sad smile. "I don't want to lose you as a friend either. All I'm saying is that I don't want to know about your little investigations anymore. I can't be part of them."

Flo was relieved by her friend's words while, at the same time, saddened by them. "I understand. I promise I won't drag you into any more adventures."

TC grimaced. "Adventures. Yeah, they're certainly that." Her smile widened. "I won't say I haven't had fun at times."

Flo nodded, sniffling. Finally, TC relented and walked over, giving Flo a hug. "I meant it when I said I still want to be friends."

"Good." Flo felt a weight lifting from her chest. "I'd better go, hun. But before I do, I've been dying to know. How in the world did you get out of that ventilation system?"

TC chuckled. "I followed it to another office where the cover was loose and shoved it off. Some poor woman was making copies when I climbed out of the wall. She'll probably never be the same again."

Flo laughed with her friend. "I'll bet. Okay. Well. I'll see you later?"

"Absolutely."

FOR THE SECOND TIME in just days, it looked like all of Silver Hills was in the lobby when Flo and Co arrived. She spotted Morty and Vlad off to one side but, as her gaze caught theirs, they turned away and ducked into the office. "Figures," she muttered under her breath. She'd nearly gotten herself and her friends killed and challenged a friendship that was important to her to save Vlad and she apparently wasn't even going to get a thank you from them in return.

Roger, Flo and Agnes joined the crowd, greeting their friends and acquaintances as they waited expectantly for Richard to make his announcement. Several moments later, the day manager emerged from the office and whistled for silence. He looked distinctly unhappy and that made Flo very nervous. "Thank you everyone, for coming down for this quick announcement. Since it directly affects each and every one of you, I wanted to make sure you heard it from me."

A soft murmur of speculation filtered through the crowd as they waited for him to go on.

Richard looked down at the sheet of paper in his hand and hesitated. When he looked up again he was frowning. "We received nearly a hundred applications for this job."

Another ripple of sound rolled through the crowd. Flo heard Agnes sigh unhappily at the news and knew that she was lamenting the fact that hers wasn't one of the apps they'd received. It was yet another bad outcome that could be laid on Flo's doorstep.

"But, although most of the applicants were distinctly unsuitable, happily for us we found the perfect person for the job."

There was another ripple of even louder murmuring. Richard waited it out. " In fact, we're so pleased with the applicant that we're foregoing the voting and we're just going to award the job."

Sound exploded as people did their best to deal with the unusual news. It was unheard of for management to take the selection out of the residents' hands. Flo realized that meant they were either shoving someone down their throats who they knew wouldn't be popular, in which case they were going to have a fight on their hands, or they'd found someone they were confident everyone would like. She slid Agnes a look and tears burned her eyes. Agnes would have fit the second scenario if she'd been given the chance.

"I'm proud and happy to announce your new weekend manager..." Richard's gaze slid over the crowd, his smile wide and clearly happy. Flo hoped that wasn't an attempt to perfume a truly ugly pig. "Agnes Willard!"

The room erupted in shouts and cheers. Agnes was immediately inundated by well-wishers, yanking her into hugs and smacking her on the back in congratulations. She quickly went from looking confused and disbelieving, to ecstatic.

Flo was crying and laughing at the same time, and when she got a chance she gave her friend a big hug.

Agnes returned the hug. "I don't understand..."

"Don't question it, hun. You and I both know you're the best person for the job and this proves Richard and the others know it too. Congratulations. You're going to be the best manager we've ever had."

Agnes sniffled, her eyes filling with happy tears as she was swept away on a tide of well-wishers.

As soon as the noise and chaos moved away, Flo turned to Roger. "I'll be back in a minute."

"Of course, doll. Do you want me to come with you?"

"No, hun. But thanks."

She hurried toward the office and opened the door. Hoping to speak to Richard, she was surprised to find only Morty and Vlad inside. The Newsome twosome stared at her for a long moment with their cold, nearly black gazes and then Morty said. "Close the door."

Feeling a flutter of trepidation, Flo did as they requested.

After a long moment of silence, Morty sighed. "I guess we owe you again."

There was no happiness in the declaration and nothing in the way of real appreciation so Flo just shrugged. "I did what was right."

Morty frowned as if the concept was a foreign one to her. "Anyway. We wanted you to know that we appreciate your help. That's why we took care of your friend."

Flo felt her eyes go wide. "You submitted that application for Agnes?"

Morty frowned as if it pained her, then jerked her head once.

"Why?"

"Because we knew it would make you happy and we do realize we owe you a debt."

Flo held Morty's gaze for a moment and then nodded. "Thanks. It means a lot to her."

Morty's grimace made it clear she couldn't care less.

Flo scanned a look toward Vlad. She hated to let him get away without thanking her himself. As it was, he was making Morty do the thanking, despite the fact he'd gotten himself into the mess with the police. But he simply held her gaze without reaction, standing so still he looked like an ugly, menacing statue.

She suddenly wanted to rip that smug look off his face. "Tell me about Melody Tyne."

Vlad flinched, his gaze skating away from hers. When he didn't respond she took a stab at it herself. "Let me guess. You hoped to throw a wrench in her lawsuit by making it appear she'd taken a job from you as a bribe. But you knew if she realized the job offer came from you she wouldn't take it so you pretended Richard offered it to her. I'm guessing she had no idea you even worked here. Am I right?"

Vlad shrugged, but she saw the truth in his eyes. He was surprised she'd put it all together.

"I hate to tell you. I met Miss Tyne and I believe your fear was a good one. If she knew you were involved she'd have never taken the job. You were going to fail."

His look turned hard. "We'll never know now, will we?"

He looked so cold and unfeeling Flo had a momentary jolt of fear that she'd helped release a guilty man. She shrugged it off. Vlad was an ass. But she didn't believe he was a killer.

Not really.

"I expect you to do what you've promised and make it right for your renters. That place you gave Agnes and I for the night was disgusting. No human being should be expected to live like that."

Morty's lips quivered. "That wasn't one of our rentals. In fact, it's been condemned by the health department. Several apartments in that complex have been set aside for total rehabbing before we can rent them."

Flo let that sink in for a minute before she spoke. "You put us in a condemned apartment?"

Vlad's thin lips stretched into a mean smile.

Morty twisted her blood-red lips to keep from grinning too.

"You people are awful."

They both shrugged. Not even attempting to dispute her assessment of them. "I don't understand. Clearly, you could care less about your renters. Why are you even bothering to fix the places up?"

"Well there's that pesky lawsuit. Despite what the ill-advised Baccarats did, the suit will go on." Morty said, grimacing. "And then there's the other thing." She looked at Vlad and lifted a brow as if to encourage him to speak.

He pulled his shoulders back and straightened, growing taller as he lifted his chin. The overhead light painted blue lines over his slicked back hair and made his widow's peak stand out in relief. "Yes, there is another reason and you might as well hear it from me."

Dread clawed at Flo's belly. She knew in that moment she wasn't going to like whatever followed. "Please don't tell me you're going to try to take the weekend manager's position away from Agnes..."

Vlad laughed meanly. "My aspirations are a bit higher than that, woman from the second floor."

She rolled her eyes. They were apparently back to that. "So, enlighten me, man from the third coffin."

Morty snorted, which was something Flo had never seen her do before. She was starting to grin, happy to have finally made the other woman laugh at one of her jokes, when Vlad's words wiped the smile right off her face.

"I was going to announce it at the vote tonight but since we won't be having one..." He frowned as if it pained him not to vote on weekend manager. "I might as well tell you now. I'm running for Mayor of Silver City."

Flo stood there gaping, completely at a loss for words.

The door opened behind her and a man came inside, closing it softly behind him. "Mr. Newsome...Mrs. Newsome," he said.

Flo turned at the sound of the deep, slightly rough voice. She felt her eyes go wide.

It was the man she'd passed the other day leaving the office. The one with the mean eyes. She suddenly realized he was also the man she and Agnes had seen Vlad greeting on the street. Up close he was even more smarmy looking than Flo had realized.

"Mrs. Bee," Vlad said in a smooth, terrifyingly normal tone of voice. "I'd like you to meet Preston Jamison. My campaign manager."

THE END

DID YOU ENJOY FLO AND Agnes's story? If so, you might want to check out the next book in the *Silver Hills Cozy Mysteries* series.

Please enjoy Chapter One of **Fowl Campaign**:

SILVER HILLS SENIOR and Singles Residence isn't exactly a boring place. Home to a death predicting cat named Tolstoy, a night manager who may or may not suck blood and float above the floor, a cook with mad voodoo and pie baking powers, and a trio of nosy sleuths who are determined to get to the bottom of the corpse in the library (maybe literally)...some might say things couldn't get any weirder.

Some would be wrong.

CHAPTER ONE

FLO, AGNES, AND CELIA stood on the sidewalk with their mouths hanging open. The big bus lumbered noisily by, its side befouled by a giant banner that said, *Vote for Vlad*, with a picture of the Silver Hills night manager's hated face.

"Why is he orange?" Agnes asked, frowning.

"They must have used spray tan to take away that undead look," Flo speculated. She shook her head as the monstrosity wound its way down Main Street and turned at the next light. "It's like we're living in an alternate universe."

Celia nodded. "I saw one of his campaign commercials this morning." She turned her frown to Flo. "It said he was Woke. What does that even mean?"

"It means his writers have poor English," Flo mused.

"Maybe it's a Vamp thing," Agnes added. "You know, beware villagers, the vampire is woke. Grab the pitchforks."

"I'm pretty sure that isn't what it means, Agnes," Celia said with a smile.

"I know one thing, I was woke too early this morning," Agnes grumbled. "I'm tired."

"The trash truck?" Flo asked. Unfortunately for Agnes, the dumpsters for the residence were right outside her window and every Tuesday they woke her up at five AM. Her friend definitely looked tired. She had purple arcs beneath her expressive gray eyes and her graying brown pageboy hairstyle was rumpled looking, as if she'd done a lot of tossing and turning.

Flo resisted the urge to smooth her own, freshly dyed blonde bouff as she gave Agnes a sympathetic look. She had shadows under her hazel eyes too. Flo's circles were from lying awake worrying about the rift between her and her friend TC.

"I'd complain again to Richard but it won't do any good," Agnes murmured.

"You're the weekend manager," Celia said quite reasonably. "Can't you make a new rule or something? Maybe request a schedule change?"

"I've tried. But Tuesday's aren't my days and Richard insists he's tried to move the time. They aren't budging."

"I think I'd be tempted to move to another apartment," Celia said. "I need my beauty sleep."

"Me too!" Agnes lamented, running her hands through the air in front of her six-foot-tall, widely-made form. "You don't think all this beauty comes easy, do you?"

Celia chuckled.

"Easily," Flo corrected. "Oh, look."

They all turned their focus across the street, where an attractive, dark-haired young woman was standing with her back to them, pretending to read a flyer that was taped to the window. She was clearly observing them in the reflection of the glass at *Cooper's Beauty Products*.

"She's watching us again," Agnes said on a frown. "It's kind of creepy."

Flo felt like crying. "TC's not creepy, Agnes. She's just struggling." Flo waved and TC ducked her head, hurrying on down the street as if she hadn't seen them.

"It's her own fault," Celia said in her customary hardline way. "She's the one keeping herself away."

"Maybe she needs to be Woke," Agnes observed, pursing her lips.

Flo started off down the street. "*Woke* my narrow behind. That's just a misuse of the language if you ask me."

"I think it means you like transvestites."

Celia and Flo stopped in their tracks and looked at Agnes in shock. "Why in the world would Vlad have a campaign commercial saying he likes transvestites?"

Agnes shrugged. "Who knows. Maybe Dave Potts is really a woman."

Potts was running against Vlad for the position of Mayor of Silver City. Since he went about three hundred pounds and had more hair on his face than most men had on their entire bodies, it seemed unlikely he was actually a woman.

"You're being ridiculous," Flo told her friend.

"I think it means you like gays," Celia offered.

"Potts could be gay," Agnes offered as they stepped off the curb and crossed the street to the Silver Hills Senior and Singles Residence.

"Even if he is," Flo countered. "Why would Vlad proclaim he liked him in a campaign commercial?"

"To grab the gay constituency, of course." Agnes said. Then she frowned. "I didn't mean that like it sounded. Though I guess Vlad could be gay too. His great, great, great ancestor was kind of Metro Sexual-ish if you ask me."

Celia, having less experience with Agnes' contorted thought processes, frowned. "Metro Sexuals aren't gay, Agnes. Well, not completely."

Flo sighed. "She's talking about Dracula."

"Ah." Celia grinned. "Vlad does kind of look like Count Dracula."

"The cereal or the actor?" Agnes asked with a grin.

Agnes and Celia shared a laugh as Flo reached for the front doors. "You two are impossible. Now, we need to sit down and figure out how to get TC back into the fold. She's breaking my heart."

Agnes veered left as soon as they came through the door, heading for the dining area, which was starting to fill up for happy hour. Several people hailed her as she strode quickly toward the big, round tables and Agnes stopped to shake hands and say a few words at every table she passed.

Celia bumped Flo's arm and chuckled. "If I didn't know better, I'd think Agnes was the one running for Mayor."

Flo's eyes widened. "Good Heavens. Don't even say such a thing in jest. Can you imagine? Her slogan would be, a pie on every table, a Twinkie in every drawer."

Celia laughed, wrapping her arm around Flo's shoulders. "Sounds good to me."

Flo had to admit to herself that Agnes would be a much better mayor than either of the people currently throwing their hat in the ring for the job.

Dave Potts was a thoroughly unlikeable fellow. He was brash and aggressive, and seemed not to care much about anything except his own rise to power and wealth. His family had a large chicken farm outside of Silver Hills, the stench of which permeated the air all through town if the wind was blowing wrong. Potts Chickens were sold across the country and he'd built up quite a business. But he'd apparently grown bored with being a Chicken King and had decided he could rule Silver City too.

Flo personally thought his crown might be a little too tight. He was so unlikeable there was little chance anybody would seriously consider him for the job. Although, given his competition, there might be a lot of nose holding happening on election day. And it wouldn't be caused by the stench of chicken poop.

Nothing needed to be said about Vladwick Newsome. A more reprehensible human being would be difficult to find. Unless one cast her gaze toward Potts.

Choosing between the two men would be a soul-crushing, psyche-scarring event that Flo was not looking forward to. She was still hoping a third candidate would surface, giving them a real choice for mayor.

"Let's go," Celia murmured in an urgent tone. "Here comes Elisa. She's heading right for us."

Elisa Kemp was Silver Hills' self-proclaimed queen of all knowledge. She knew everything about everybody and if she didn't know something, she knew how to get the information. Flo had found the woman's busy-body network handy a time or two when trying to solve a crime, but as a social acquaintance, Elisa was a bit hard to take.

Flo never knew when Elisa's rumor-fed mind was targeting *her* life for future information sharing. It was an occupational hazard for Flo since she'd decided to become a private investigator of sorts. One that she knew she had to embrace, no matter what it cost. She flicked her fingers toward Agnes, across the room. "You go on, Ce. I'll talk to Elisa and see what she wants. Maybe she's heard something about a new candidate for mayor." *Hope springs eternal*, Flo mused to herself.

Celia patted her on the back and hurried away, anxious to avoid the sour, snoopy Elisa.

Flo smiled as the woman hurried up to her, her trademark hangdog expression plastered across her narrow face. She reached cold, bony fingers to Flo, clasping her hands quickly before dropping them. "I have news about the mayoral race."

Flo let her excitement show in her expression, feeding the other woman's ego. "Please tell me there's going to be a third candidate."

Elisa blinked, her gaze tightening with pique. "How would I know that, Flo?"

How did the woman know anything? Flo asked herself. "Oh, I'm sorry, I thought when you said you had news..."

Elisa pursed her thin lips, flapping her hands in the air between them. As always, she reminded Flo of an enormous praying mantis with pincers for lips. "Flo, listen to me. This is important."

Flo's mouth slammed shut and she clasped her hands in front of her, giving Elisa her patient teacher look.

The other woman's hand swept over a loose, gray-black strand of hair on her temple, smoothing it back into the over-tight bun at the nape of her long neck.

She hunched her Ichabod Crane-like form and lowered her head toward Flo, her breath tinged with garlic from her lunch of spaghetti and meatballs. "Dave Potts needs to see you."

Flo blinked "Really? Why? I barely know the man." Flo was pretty sure she'd taught Potts's sons a decade earlier, when she'd worked as a substitute school teacher. She'd met his wife a few times but couldn't recall having met the candidate face to face, except maybe in passing at a school event.

Elisa shrugged bony shoulders. "I have no idea. I got word through my grapevine that he's trying to contact you. Apparently, he's called here a few times and Vlad's hung up on him."

Flo frowned. "I hope he's not looking for dirt on Vlad. I don't like the man, but I'm not going to insert myself into this race. The two men will need to sink or swim without me."

But Elisa was shaking her head. The errant strand of hair flew from the bun again, yearning to be free. "I don't think that's it. Beatrice Barker overheard Vlad demanding to know what Potts wanted with you. She inferred from Vlad's side of the conversation that Potts wouldn't tell him."

"Oh my!" Flo breathed out. Then it hit her. "Potts wants to hire me as an investigator?"

"It seems that way, yes." Elisa's expression turned sly. "Is there any kind of—erm—finder's fee or anything?"

Flo barely kept from rolling her eyes. "Don't get ahead of yourself, Elisa. Let me talk to the man. If he ends up hiring me I'll cut you in for a small fee." Though it sounded as if she should be paying the fee to Beatrice Barker instead.

Elisa's pincer lips tightened. "How small?"

"We'll discuss it later." Flo started to turn away and then realized she needed to keep Elisa in her corner. She bit back a sigh, turning to offer the other woman a tight smile. "Thanks for bringing this to me, Elisa."

Elisa nodded. "You'll keep me informed?"

"Absolutely. Bye now."

Flo hurried toward the group surrounding Agnes at their usual table. It was a lively group, filled with several of the younger residents from the singles side of the building. But Flo wasn't interested in joining the throng. She was making a bee-line toward Bea Barker.

VISIT THE SILVER HILLS book page on Sam's website for more information and purchase links!

https://samcheever.com/books/#SilverHills

WHAT'S NEXT?

READ MORE OF SAM'S Work: Did you enjoy the book? If you'd like to read more books like this from Sam Cheever, check out her other bestselling books:

Silver Hills Cozy Mysteries: https://samcheever.com/books/#SilverHills

Country Cousin Mysteries: https://samcheever.com/books/#Country

Gainfully Employed Mysteries: https://samcheever.com/books/#gainfully

Grave Theatrics Mysteries: https://samcheever.com/books/#grave

Enchanting Inquiries Mysteries: https://samcheever.com/books/#enchanting

Provide Reviews: If you enjoy the books, please consider showing support for Sam by leaving reviews so that other readers will know what to expect from a Sam Cheever book. Book reviews help readers as well as authors!

Connect: If you'd like to stay up to date on Sam's News, Releases and Appearances, consider liking her Facebook Page, following her on Twitter, and signing up for her Newsletter:

Newsletter: https://samcheever.com/newsletter/

Website: https://www.SamCheever.com

Blog: https://samcheever.com/blog/

Facebook: https://www.facebook.com/SamCheever-Author

Bookbub: https://www.bookbub.com/authors/sam-cheever

Goodreads: https://www.goodreads.com/author/show/1812031.Sam_Cheever

ABOUT THE AUTHOR

USA TODAY AND WALL Street Journal Bestselling Author Sam Cheever writes mystery and suspense, creating stories that draw you in and keep you eagerly turning pages. Known for writing great characters, snappy dialogue, and unique and exhilarating stories, Sam is the award-winning author of 100+ books.

To learn more about Sam and her work, visit her at one of her online hotspots:

Website[1] | Facebook[2] | Goodreads[3] | Blog[4]

---

1. http://www.samcheever.com/

2. https://www.facebook.com/pages/Sam-Cheever-Author/102117321982

3. http://www.goodreads.com/author/show/1812031.Sam_Cheever

4. http://samcheever.com/blog